CHANNEL SWIMMER

Thanks so much
for coming to
the launch!

Ulrike Draesner

CHANNEL SWIMMER

A Novel

Translated from the German
by Rebecca Braun

Upper West Side Philosophers, Inc.
New York

Published by Upper West Side Philosophers, Inc.,
New York, NY 10025, USA
www.westside-philosophers.com / www.yogaforthemind.us

Library of Congress Cataloging-in-Publication Data

Names: Draesner, Ulrike, 1962- author. | Braun, Rebecca, translator.
Title: Channel swimmer : a novel / Ulrike Draesner ; translated from the
German by Rebecca Braun.
Other titles: Kanalschwimmer. English
Description: New York : Upper West Side Philosophers, Inc., 2025.
Identifiers: LCCN 2024041732 (print) | LCCN 2024041733 (ebook) | ISBN
9781935830818 (paperback) | ISBN 9781935830825 (hardback) | ISBN
9781935830832 (ebook)
Subjects: LCGFT: Novels.
Classification: LCC PT2664.R324 K3613 2025 (print) | LCC PT2664.R324
(ebook) | DDC 833/.92--dc23/eng/20241023
LC record available at https://lccn.loc.gov/2024041732
LC ebook record available at https://lccn.loc.gov/2024041733
Typsetting and Design: UWSP, Inc.

Cover Design: UWSP, Inc.
Cover Image: Detail adapted from Uehara Konen, Hato zu (ca. 1910;
https://www.loc.gov/resource/jpd.01826/ • Library of Congress, Prints &
Photographs Division, Repr. # LC-DIG-jpd-01826)
Author Photograph © by Jürgen Bauer

Fresh, yellow-tinged light fell through the leaves of the thicket in front of the kitchen window onto the floor and table.

The cadences of a Chopin étude were tinkling through the ceiling. Friday afternoon. Maude's piano lesson. He had taken the train from his lab in Oxford to Paddington, from there it was another thirty minutes on the tube. Weekends were for coming home. That's what his wife had called 8 Portland Terrace from the very first day: home. They had been living here for a year.

He needed a cup of tea.

Something about the kitchen wasn't right.

It was a basement room, like in many Victorian houses. Hanging his coat – they were in the grip of a hot spell in the middle of July, but even still the usual downpours and irritating gusts of wind fanned up the Thames from the North Sea – hanging his coat over the chair by the door, he saw that someone had turned the magnet upside down on the fridge. The red double decker bus was lying on its roof, its wheels lurching up into the air. Instead of the usual shopping list, it clasped a letter.

Oxford, 12 November, 1978

Dearest Maude,

... anyone else but you ... can no longer ...

Abigail ...

5

… under Silas'
dressing gown …
            … forgotten those days on Sylt?
But to you at least … The way those days ended …
            … We had to deal with things that
just a few hours earlier we didn't …
    … because life as a …
        … make some decisions …
                        … free …
        … without any lies …
    … I had to tell you …
        … Maude …
Forever yours,
Charles

They were cuckoo.

They: His wife and her lover.

His wife and his best friend.

Maude and Silas.

The water boiled up blue in the gauge on the kettle. Chopin beat 1, 2, 3, 1, 2, 1, 2. Without a moment's thought, his hand had pocketed the page. He saw himself sitting in his student digs; the fire in the hearth – two elements, like a toaster – glowed red, the butter that he kept on the sill inside the pointed gothic window was stubbornly hard. His fountain pen had scratched its way over the paper. Forty years old, that letter.

He added milk to his tea.

He looked at the plastic spoon. Plastic didn't get hot.

A bit crowded, his marriage.

Crowded, with the three of them.

In his, Charles', new London house.

Please touch, says the sign. The room is buzzing with the sound of people. The draft makes two dinosaur skeletons sway gently on their supports; one whale's jawbone has been leaned against a pillar.

He travels so often between the two cities on the Thames, capitals of finance and education, respectively, that he is thankful for every day he doesn't have to spend on one of the rickety trains, for every day that he doesn't arrive at the dingey Oxford platform and have to climb with hundreds of other passengers over the pedestrian bridge pieced together out of the thinnest of strips of metal. And yet there he had been, back on the train again, late yesterday evening.

He had spent the night in his *pied-à-terre*. The flat is close to several acres of wild meadow where cows and horses graze. It's been four thousand years, or so they say, since this was ploughed; now joggers and dogs chase over the sandy paths. In summertime it smells of cow pats and he can barely believe where he lives. How it can be so rural – grassy, moist and warm, full of insects – and then he walks just ten minutes and finds himself in his lab, or in a museum like this one.

Five whales, the smallest an ancestor of the porpoise, the largest a bottlenose whale, are hanging from the silver-grey ribs of the ceiling. Oxford's home for natural history is warm and echoey, with mighty iron girders carrying the glass roof, an ark of God's creation flying through the air, a dream of infinity clad in a crinoline of Victorian engineering. One hundred feet above, skeletal heads protrude from neck vertebrae the size of armchairs, oversized, pointy mandibles travel like sledges on their sharp, bony blades through the air, while the feet of the 65 million-year-old dinosaurs spread their powerful toes wide right where he is standing.

His fist fits into the cavity of the missing tooth in the whale's jawbone. *Don't touch, fragile.*

As a student, he had lived in College accommodation, then rented in the USA and also later, with Maude, in Germany. The terraced house with its imposing black door is their first, English home. He bought it for its kitchen, for that slopey, underwater light. Maude found some better reasons for the bank. In his job he counts cells, "unlocking the secret of life," as his department's banner proclaims on each Open Day. Still five years to go in his job, incredible that they had wanted him back.

He strolls through the rows of unusual and extinct animals, past Charles Darwin and Double-Helix Watson. Creatures are clambering about between water and rock. Crawling ashore. Looking at him through oversized eyes. Flying dinosaurs, slender as lizards: it's a shame that these no longer stalk the planet (perhaps they had angled their legs like chameleons, making careful splashes as they went? – he can't help thinking of cold macaroni). How strange it would be to meet them on his next twilight walk in the Cotswolds, along with a rabbit jumping out of the hedge or a herd of deer crossing to a copse. Dinosaurs are relatives of birds, says the sign, originally quite delicately built, and for a few seconds that's how reality strikes him: a cute and agile jumping dinosaur, fashioned out of habits and assumptions, always slipping away just when you think you've got a hold of it. His letter, as if it were a shopping list, clipped to the fridge door with the up-ended double-decker.

Oxford, November 1978: Dearest Maude.

Ink, his old Montblanc.

For the dinosaurs, forty years is nothing, for Oxford almost nothing, for a life quite a lot; for Charles' time with Maude, everything.

Under different circumstances he would have been pleased to find she had kept the letter. He knows, of course, why she had to dig up these lines now that Silas is back on the scene. Silas, the longstanding English friend, who used to call in on them regularly when he was travelling through Düsseldorf in between business trips. Silas no longer seems to be travelling much. Does he even still have his flat in Bloomsbury, or has he already moved in with them? With Maude?

Charles' face isn't burning with shame. No shame sits on his shoulders.

Nor is he even there. He has run away. As if he were a novice in marriage. Uninitiated in crises. And yet, for forty years everything had been fine.

Nothing is burning with shame; instead shame has formed a clump, a clot rolling around between his ribs.

The master builder folded the aisles of the museum into the centre and pushed the whole building together into a triangle of pointed glass, so that the light is free to fulfil its mechanical duty and shine like clear crystal on the collected animals below – of which now only the hominids roam. Even on Saturdays, children in navy pullovers with purple edging around the neck, the girls in short navy skirts and knee-length socks that always leave a strip of skin, are guided up and down the aisles, as if being woven into the material of evolution themselves. "What is life on earth?" "Where do you come from?" "What is normal?"

Once again, he is amazed by just how much the city's environs are full of fossils: frozen dinosaur footprints, gigantic hipbones, the skulls that belong to them looking like they are from chickens: comparatively fragile and fine. Moving *en masse*, those fern-eating and shell-crunching beauties, those inventions of primeval mud, beasts with small brains and first sets of lungs, crazy creatures from the water, revolutionaries from the air, lugubrious pioneers of walking, those first and most deep-rooted ancients of the planet pushed forth from their territory, the swamp.

We'll find a home for you too, Maude had said, when they had moved back from Düsseldorf to England after three decades on the continent. He no longer recognised this country where he, Charles had grown up and where she, Maude, belonged. Completely, she said. And so did he, Charles!

Half, he said.

A home for Maude. For Maude's English self.

Standing in the museum shop at one end of the palatial hall full of skeletons that was designed to look like a glasshouse, and searching, out of habit, for a present for her, he finds himself face to face with the white rabbit from Alice in Wonderland.

Trinkets, souvenirs are for sharing a time when you weren't together. What is the point of them when you don't share any time together anymore?

He stares at the rabbit and tries to remember the scientific word for "stuffed."

A determined looking man stares back at him in the shop's glass partition, a little akin to a bird himself, with some strand of hair always sticking up and beady round eyes hiding behind his half-frame reading glasses. He thinks he looks like a crow who's been given a wire clothes hanger. Make yourself a nest out of that! Maude loved animal documentaries. She had shown him that clip, latterly.

Inside him, something is missing. He has given up listening to music, maybe because his wife is teaching piano. Oh come on! Not even he believes this for a second. They had agreed to time apart, in the first instance. He longs for Maude, has rediscovered what this means. Light falls through the hall, the glass of a previous century, conceived at the end of the one before that, a dream of unity and harmony, when the world, cloaked in the belief that man can know everything about nature, wanted to sparkle. This was a knowledge gleaned by killing animals and sticking coloured, molten quartz sand into their skulls for eyes. Now he counts chemical elements and the passage of time in cellular processes triggered by visual stimuli on a screen. How long does it take to click on "yes," "no," or "continue"?

He likes Silas. He knows him. Silas, his toughest opponent, his training partner in Camden Swimming Club, always driving him on, always there for him.

He gathers himself once more, passes the smallest of the dinosaurs, fragile and in need of as much care as a primeval plant that, reduced to its skeleton, is but a pattern of itself.

Until something catches his eye and an idea begins to take shape in his own body as he lingers in front of the board that depicts them crawling onto land. Dripping, solid, eyes agog.

He stands under the smallest one, looks, from behind, right into the depths of all their ribcages. Held by invisible wires, the five whale skeletons float under the ceiling, as if they were chasing one another in order of size through the air. Nose to tail they are racing along, the bony trail of an invisible plan. The beige-yellow mandible of the middle one, bent like a tuning fork, almost seems to vibrate from the body warmth rising up from all the visitors below. Charles practically feels like a ghost himself, hidden on the bed of an icy ocean, watching the secret flight of a group of sea spirits. For a few sublime seconds, he even thinks he can hear their voices in the crystal clarity of midday. With their long, sharp, bony mouths the whales are cutting through the airy ocean of time and singing with the blood of their lungs what it means not to be who you seem.

1

White horses: the wind blowing smack against the tide, distinct waves, their crests beaten white with froth.

Through the mist the rising sun was casting fiery fingers. Silver-edged tufts of cloud hung well below the zenith, but still high over the Channel. Green and grey, constantly stirring up sand, the water threw the falling light back out into a sky that was gradually turning blue. All around the cliff-top where Charles was doing his stretches the world rose easily into the day.

Sea swell, type one: the wind blowing with the tide, over the water, pushing the waves out in long lines. Brendan, Charles' life insurance, the ship's captain and an officially recognised source of information on this shimmering sheet, deemed such desirable conditions an "improbability." The reality was type three: choppy seas. The wind was blowing side-on against the tidal current, significant swell, freak waves, sea-sickness. Oh yes, for the swimmer too. Particularly for the swimmer. *Do you mind?*

06:30 a.m. The cliff-top restaurant was serving instant coffee and soggy toast. Britain. This was where it began, this was where it ended.

"I don't think you should take whitener," said the old man to the older of his two female companions.

All three were sitting at the wooden table diagonally across from Charles. The one with the lilac pullover, walking stick, and a view out onto the glistening artery said, "My teeth are excellent," and dipped her oat biscuit into the hot drink. "White horses today, the sea!"

At this time of day only seagulls, old people and swimmers were awake. The birds, creatures whose veins coursed with blood, not tea, had hidden themselves in crannies in the cliff but were still making the usual racket. Barely perceptible vertical streaks were hanging between the water and the sky: a loneliness dashed with rivulets.

The path down to the beach started at the benches. Charles put his phone into his coat pocket so as to fall more easily into a stride. According to the Real-Life-Crossing app, Brendan's ship, the *Henry*, was heading back into Dover Port after that night's successful swim. The next candidate on the list was him. Throw up, shiver, carry on front-crawl – be a swimmer. A swimmer amongst mega-tankers, ferries, yachts, cruise-ships in the world's busiest waterway. A swimmer wearing nothing more than trunks, goggles and a cap, a head gasping for air, directed and fed by an accompanying boat for the fourteen or seventeen or twenty-five hours it would take to cross the strait, the artery, the plume.

To the left and right of him the vertical cliffs towered stubbornly against the sky, gigantic chalks, boards pushed together. England's end, England's beginning. A home for you too, Maude had said. He jogged sure-footedly over the stony ground between the empty expanses. Should he send his wife a piece of chalk before he swam out? Black veins of flint between the crumbly white lumps, his final letter! Beautiful pathos. The piece that came away when he knocked the edge of his hand a couple of times against the cliff looked like a mole's snout. Blind in all its white.

The chunk of chalk bounced off down the steep, stony path, out of sight. The swims from that morning popped up one after the other on the websites of the two Channel-crossing clubs. He would be fed from a rod, like a zoo animal. They would open and attach a tube of energy gel to the gripper, pineapple or lemon flavour. Pineapple makes your lips sticky straight away. Last year, a swimmer had merrily injected the stuff down his throat each and every hour with an oversized syringe. It was so harmlessly funny that this summer's set of hopefuls couldn't stop talking about it on the beach. The syringe grew with every telling; something had to come from being by the sea.

Finally.

Le fin, the end. Or whatever this Channel was.

Under no circumstances was the candidate allowed to touch the feeding rod.

Charles had stocked up with strawberry, peach, vanilla.

His pilot would pack flat cola for his stomach, ginger biscuits, peppermint tea. *Pilot*: it made Charles think of wings. The majority of crossings failed either because of the weather or the food. Each feed shouldn't take longer than one minute; over the length of the crossing that still added up to forty-five minutes of lost time. He had no interest in breaking any records. He wanted to make it = touch = onto land.

You used an equals sign at the end of experiments, to tot up rows, to finalize bills. Three quarters of an hour = one and a half to two hours in the freezing cold, swimming against the current, thanks to tidal drift.

It's the drift against your physical strength plus wind plus "your mind," Brendan had said. The latter was his chance to get equal.

Ultimately, or, in the end: the sea. Fish, already caught, grew between your hands here, the waters and the skies filled up with shadowy shapes, the air pushed and rushed, its whisperings unfathomable. Even at this early hour a family had already set up camp in the sandy bay of the otherwise pebbly beach. Two adults in hoodies and blankets were feeling their short night. Their two toddlers, half naked and still so small that they hadn't yet forgotten what swimming was, were feeling and hearing God knows what.

Tomorrow, he wanted to be on his way by the time the sun was this high in the sky, tomorrow, or at the very latest the day after tomorrow, preferably right now. He had been training for over a year, following a strict plan of cold-water winter swims in the river to toughen up and then every weekend from May onwards in the port of Dover. Now, in the middle of August, the Channel had reached its maximum temperature: 17.2 degrees Celsius.

The Channel, the soup, the filthy brew.

He almost tripped over the boy in the teddy bear suit who was poking around in a pile of seaweed and gleefully shouting "Easter egg!" as he held a piece of plastic tight with both hands. A fat face, dirty mouth. Charles fell into a trot. Children didn't look for shells anymore. They wanted to scratch polystyrene, chew pieces of foil. The clouds were dangling directly overhead like fleecy coats torn from the sea. Artificial fur, grinning foam. Reality kept changing every second.

He was sixty-two, working on his last big research project, and slowly having to think about making himself replaceable. When he wasn't in the lab time passed sluggishly, now that he no longer lived in the kitchen bathed in underwater light. Thirteen months had passed since he had moved out of Portland Terrace. He had picked stuff up there on a couple of occasions, always by prior arrangement. Sometime in the autumn Silas had sent a message: let's meet for a beer. Fifty-five years of Silas, thirty-seven years of marriage to Maude, one beer.

The Channel had saved him. A training schedule, measurable signs of improvement not in a set of experiments, not in his students' careers, but in him. Where he was unquestionably himself: in his muscles, pulse, fat.

Brendan had taught him to read sea charts. The Channel – *La Manche* had five strips: English territory, the southwest shipping lane, the separation zone, the northeast shipping lane, French territory. The "motorways" left and right of Z, the no-man's land, were each about six miles wide. Containerships, giant cruise-ships, freighters and ferries. The southwest lane went along the English coast and out into the Atlantic, its counterpart on the French side ended in the North Sea. Jellyfish billowed everywhere, huge shoals of them, lone stragglers, transverse floaters, nature's revenge. Jellyfish, particularly the stinging kind, were having an exceptionally good year.

He slung a pebble in the direction of the water. Because of the strong tidal currents, his route had to be planned in two loops; usually a third was added during the crossing, around the grey nose, Cap Griz-Nez, where French land finally seemed to come towards the English swimmer. This was where every cold-water hero wanted to finish up and just about no-one did. A dense, grey fog had descended on the cliffs. Brooding formations raced overhead, seemingly devoid of depth, as if in a time-lapse videoclip: sinister, comical.

20.7 miles, the narrowest point, island and continent as close as they come. Grease was permitted. Buy the maxi pot from the Varne Ridge Caravan Park. Fifty percent lanolin, fifty percent Vaseline.

Trunks, goggles, cap.

Bare shoulders, that's the rule.

So you really ... don't mind?

The younger channel crossers made sure that their pilot posted a snap every fifteen minutes and scribbled the real-time responses from their friends on a whiteboard. Charles wasn't going to feed his modicum of aquatic authenticity into the Net. He needed it for himself.

Maude: "You don't mind, do you?"

Silas: "C'mon, old chap. The three of us."

He had imagined a relaxing retirement: writing his book, travelling for lectures, spending more time with Maude.

And then she had taken everything out of his control, with a smile. It was so easy. And not even the smile was for him.

When did a future collapse?

Silently, in any case.

The next stone – he threw it at a gull – glinted. So, the sun had shone for a moment? Sometimes you only noticed the sun in England when the drizzle started up again. This was as ridiculous as his domestic situation.

Not to forget: the noise. He had reached Dover's port. A sky full of planes landing was stretched tight over water and town. Decades of lull. Ships' captains, crews, and swimmers staring out to sea; hotel owners, B&B hosts and pub landlords staring at them staring. Each group talked about the weather and hoped to confound the other. Crockery clattered, the wind rattled at the windows. To stop their teeth chattering, the swimmers stamped their way over the Swimmers' Beach at the end of the marina, knocking the gravel stones in all directions, and slapped Vaseline on every inch of bare skin they could find. Candidates, their helpers and veterans met up in the White Horse in the afternoons and evenings. Here the walls bore carvings, as if they were chalky rocks: the date of the crossing, the swimmer's name, motto.

"Mr Charles!" Mr Prim's voice was noiselessly followed by Mr Prim, a short man with an enormous nose that was so bulbous and red he might as well have boiled it every morning in the water for his tea. Charles took a cup with extra sugar because he was a man, or maybe just a human being, and he needed something sweet. Prim sprinkled in two spoonfuls. "For you, love!"

Love! Charles was a love, candidate, mouse. You were on first-name terms here, that was enough.

You presented yourself. As body.

Everything else you kept under wraps.

A matter of "life and death." "Right to the limit," etc. The phrases were reeled off for the press, the Net. Your mind fell into a lull before the swim, and yes, by all means, in the week, no, the years after it, or so smirked the veterans. The clichés couldn't capture what it felt like in any case.

Charles slurped. That wasn't allowed when Maude (= noise sensitive) was at the table, but here it seemed okay. The day's first mouthful of tea. When he looked back up, the beach was soft, the channel a gurgling blue. Spider-leg shafts of sunlight warmed his arms. Yes, this was the morning: the water and the skies loosened their connection, a space opened up for people and tea and seagulls addicted to tea. Foam-white, the beak a luminous plastic yellow, one of them landed next to his foot. Mr Prim topped up his cup, the seagull watched attentively, and – boom!

You had to be deaf not to hate her; and yet most people loved her. Freda, the Queen! She was a mythical figure, root-ed in history. She was also town, beach, and fame into the bargain. And practical: a rectangle who knew how to roll, wrapped in a purple-grey fleece, enveloped in the smell of cigarettes. Her training group followed at a respectful dis-tance: FORCE (Freda's Organ of Robust Coercive Exercise). The edges of her face swam out wide, while her nose and eyes pulled in towards one another. Her mouth went both ways, pursed in the middle, wide as a fish all around, liable to rup-ture at any moment.

Freda's mouth was hers by design. It was new. Loudly it – or rather, she – counted her recruits into the sea. And later, much later, back out again. That was how you did it here. The queen of the beach, volunteer and self-appointed swim-ming aide, mother of crossings, whipped out an electric ket-tle, poured flasks of tea in a flash, shouted "cup a pound" across the wind-blown sand and destroyed Mr. Prim with one short sideways glance. She also rented out towels. Businesswoman, shepherd, charity worker all in one. And that white thing over there on the right, behind the port wall, must be the *Henry*? In 1990, Freda's daughter had crossed the blue artery three times without stopping: front crawl to France, turn around, front crawl to England, turn around, front crawl to Calais. Swim, stagger, shit, thirty-four hours and forty minutes, *your Mum's so proud of you!*

A young seagull hacked at Freda's grease jar with its beak. Result: panicked flapping, seagull in headstand, legs and tail in the air, beak stuck fast. Laughter sprang from mouth to mouth, swelled along the beach. Freda grabbed the creature by the belly, freed it from its vertical, head-first dive, sacrificed a towel and wiped clean the beak of the perplexed bird.

"Even the dumbest gull will only do that once."

"That's Darwin, live!"

The FORCE clapped, the bird staggered off. Charles was feeling better by the minute. Freda's new lips were made of silicon, a light "natural" pink. Of course he bought a cuppa from her; in return, she stuck out her bottom lip to let him see the seam.

The sea breeze had eaten away her old lips. Gradually, over the years. Because everything here did what it could do best.

The engine of the *Henry* would chug to the best of its ability, as would the wind whistle, the sea slap, break, roar, or what have you.

And what did he want?

Freda's hands waved about under his nose: he, Charly, didn't have a clue about nuffink. Oh, they would stretch out their vicious, crooked claws and wring his Vaseline-smeared neck, so they would!

"Who?"

Oh, wasn't he a sweetie?!

Them? The voices, she said, the hallucinations, the submerged egos! Don't you know? That's what Freda said, the Grand Mother of Lore and Legend – and you had to have your wits about you with all those mermaids, sirens, women. Just like the sea.

The Channel looked small on maps, little more than a country lane, a narrow vessel, a silver worm. But on the beach it was widely known that you were crawling your way up Mount Everest. Except it was further (= Darwin live).

More than three people a day reached the top of the eight-thousand metre mountain; the Channel was crossed by a maximum of eighty solo swimmers a year. Almost every season yielded fatalities, even when the protocol was strictly enforced and you were not allowed to set out without an accompanying boat. How the chalks were sparkling now! The tangle of rocks hanging askew made the morning sky over the town well up into a blister.

Do you mind?

He had placed his shoes on the mat, stroked Sampo, the Setter. The door to the sitting room was ajar and he saw them on the sofa, nestled together behind a Notebook. Compared to her nose and mouth, Maude's forehead and chin were small. Her wavy hairline was what softened and rounded it out into a pretty face. He could still sense how slumped he had stood there, the doorknob in his right hand, only half a body seeing half bodies. Maude had pushed her bare feet (she never wore socks at home) under Silas' thighs. The two of them were practising, so the story went, for a concert, they were listening to music, chatting. Charles hung around in his lab for most of the week and, when he came home, he smelled of chemicals. Or so Maude said. For a long time he thought her cheerfulness was a cover for the fact she was missing Hazel, who had stayed in Germany. While he was working in Oxford, Maude was sitting here alone in the house all week. An empty nest. He'd figured this one out nicely. She hadn't been missing a thing!

Silas' oboe was resting on the piano. A body for fingers, a body with keys and a rod system. Maude had blossomed in London. Immediately, Silas' friends had welcomed her and her music into their circle. With a kiss to the hand. She had kept on telling him that. The Brits leaving Europe didn't bother her. She had had her time on the Continent, she said. Charles had disagreed, this couldn't just be all about her. Well, actually, it was high time it was, his wife had retorted, she was sixty: "it's my turn now."

That time when he stood in the doorway, she hadn't noticed him. Only Silas' eyes watched him retreat.

Were the two sleeping together? Did that even matter anymore? When they were twenty, the jealousy had been obvious: the love, the exclusivity, the shame. When they were twenty everything had been simple.

And now, half a life later? Should he be scared?

He was scared.

But of what?

Maude called her new life "being-at-home." Silas popped round during the week. Charles saw less of him than before the move back to England. He felt his presence. When a towel was hanging over the side of the bath, or the armchair standing in the bay on the first floor so that you could put your feet on the sill and smoke out the window. But, above all, he sensed his friend on his wife. He smelled him on her. Maude smelled more like the Maude-of-old again. Sometimes Charles wanted to pinch his nose; it was as if his faculties were deceiving him.

"Ah," said Freda. No apparition, this woman. She had been looking out over the Channel with him. A ring of smoke rose from her mouth. "The world has brandished its whip."

A pause. A smoke-ring. The semi-crustacean at his side extinguished her cigarette and smiled.

Candidate sure.

Brendan, on the phone. His personal sea dog with the figure to match: short, stocky, hairy. Only the bass voice was missing. It was as if the sun had not only bleached the pilot's eyes (light blue), but also ratcheted his voice skywards. They had already been over everything, but now they had to repeat the process, that was the protocol. "So why do you want to do the swim?"

Brendan, soon to be Charles' only friend for twenty-four hours, his biggest enemy (= if he pulled him out of the water before he had made it to France, if he didn't let him finish his attempt), Brendan was waiting.

Call it a flight of fancy. All of his own.

That wasn't a reason. It was two already.

"Just my thing!" Charles shouted into the air, addressing the empty patch where the end of the receiver used to hang.

The path led through mixed forest, slippery, the chalk cheating on you. As part of the training programme, Charles had taken up lodgings outside of Dover, halfway to Folkestone, where he ran up and down the cliffs at least twice a day. Sometimes he swam with the others in the port in the morning, but today he wanted to have breakfast in his B&B. Afterwards he would read, sleep, go for a second run. There was to be no more swimming now, so close to the crossing. He had to protect his shoulders, tendons, skin.

Captain Webb had been deaf for a week after the crossing. Surrounded by journalists, on the ninth day he put on record that swimming the forty miles had left his legs a little stiff. He didn't mention all the raw flesh around his neck. People had entertained daft notions of bravery back then. They still did.

The railway line ran between the cliffs and the Channel, with an iron bridge allowing pedestrians to cross. Charles climbed. On the opposite horizon the French coast was so clear and fine as if the sun, now fully risen, had hatched it on the other side of the Earth overnight and just set it down here to harden.

The Channel. Devil's shit. Silas' face.

Silas, owner of Chang & Barnes, Tea Incorporate. Silas Incorporate, best friend, fellow swimmer, reappeared in Düsseldorf ten years ago. Silas, a Leo, his once blonde mane still thick, the kind of person who would walk into a room and radiate warmth. Silas was English, and therefore not loud, luminous rather, emanating subtlety and wit, a piece of home for him, Charles, too. Maude kindled the fire in the hearth on the Rhine, Silas sent cards for the mantelpiece, brought sweets and classic novels for Hazel, the daughter of the house. Maude read the novels; even Charles took up Dickens. On Sundays they would serve an English roast for their guest, Maude would bake scones or pies, and Silas started to travel via Frankfurt ever more frequently when undertaking one of his many Asian tea trips, telling them about England and binding Charles and Maude back into their past. He was careful only to mention the things they might miss. The rolling skies. That very British embarrassment. Victoria Sponge, its jam and cream filling as sweet as the eternal queen's lost empire. The wind that really was an eternal force.

Silas was horribly talented. He brought Marmite with him, making Maude roll her eyes and discover that she *still* liked the stuff. Silas, half a head taller than Charles and even as a seventeen-year-old five inches broader across the chest. Silas, the child without a mother, nevertheless had had a home, a father who cared for him, who went on holiday with his son and exchanged the parquet floors of London's stock exchange for a villa in the Cevennes in time to avoid a heart attack. Charles' own father, by contrast, was an ambitious but also in many ways anxious man, held out for his second heart attack and died wearing a suit and muttering figures at the age of fifty-three (the stock market had been his world, Charles had not shared it with him). Silas, who seemed to have navigated the years so unscathed that Charles grew jealous, Silas who meanwhile was good at something that had previously escaped him = now he could laugh at himself with infectious good humour. All of which made Silas *ever more charming* and culminated (damn it) in a Silas who was already back playing oboe with Maude in Düsseldorf, as if she and he had never stopped.

Playing and noting, in a quasi-aside, "You always meet twice in life, isn't that what the Germans say?"

Silas, in short, the English invasion. Long ago, Charles had paid a high price to be rid of this man who was sitting now in his living room, making family life very pleasant. Hazel and Silas' daughter became friendly with one another and visited Silas' father, Tex, in his villa in Levain, where a caterpillar farm had given way to a repair workshop for wind instruments. Maude listened, Maude waited, listened ever more attentively. He had underestimated the extent to which she lived by her ear: sounds, tones, words. Soon she was looking at photos, clicking her way on the Internet through London's massively overheated housing market and revealed to the family – Maude of all people, the one who had "made herself at home" in Germany, as Hazel put it, Maude, who spoke the most beautiful German of them all, the kind with an unbeatable British accent – revealed to them, and Silas was sitting there too, that she wanted to go back to the English capital. Had spent enough of her life on the Continent. Even missed driving on the left!

"And me?" he had stammered.

"You'll see to it."

A year later they moved. For Charles it all happened at deafening speed. "Out of nowhere." His finances took a hit – from industry back into academia. His old university accepted him back, even seemed pleased, but it did mean he would have to commute between Oxford and London. When they had viewed Portland Terrace Maude had cuddled into

27

Charles, said she was glad he had relented. There was talk of equals and joy. Then she said the sentence about home.

When it came to it, Charles coped with the situation better than expected. For over a hundred years both his maternal and paternal ancestors had moved across Europe, sometimes making their fortune, sometimes losing their way, sometimes of their own accord, sometimes under duress. They had been adventure-seeking for sure, also melancholic, nervous. Perhaps he had inherited some of that as wanderlust. Maude was harder to move from the spot; she had only left England on Charles' account – well, before that she had set out to Vienna on her own accord and now she wanted to go back to please herself too, apparently. But that sentence about home annoyed him. What made her think that Düsseldorf hadn't been a home to him? That he didn't feel at home in England?

He sped up down the last part of the chalk path. The cliff faces, covered in notches and cracks, stood sheer against the startlingly blue morning. Bees hummed their way among the woody coastal vegetation, tits shot like feather balls from one bush to the next, the wind repeatedly grabbing them by their plumage.

Was he seeking out the Channel like some great physiological comfort blanket?

An absurd enchantment?

The air gurgled, whistled. The sea crashed about, the sun noiselessly wandered on its way, an illusion caused by the emptiness of space. The withered, bare stems of a tall, black-seeded weed that he couldn't identify lay at the top of the cliff, growing almost horizontally out of the ground. The stems were bending right down with the wind, lifting themselves back up again. The driving, slamming gusts kept getting stronger.

At 12:40 p.m. the tide had turned. Pushing deceptively real machine guns up to their cheeks, they stood in front of a screen the size of a wall: a heavy woman, an ageing cowboy, their tender-limbed child. The arcade was heaving, rocky tunes, commercial. The town felt run down, only the weather reliably on top form, ahead of its forecast, so to speak. No sooner did a rare finger of sunlight penetrate the clouds and the two-legged creatures would come rushing from their caves. Whoever could, grabbed an instrument and busked. A chowder of music spewed over the port of England's narrowest sea.

He bought himself a broad-brimmed straw hat, baggy shorts in peacock blue, plastic sliders. Short, grey-haired, his reflection stood in the mirror of the changing room. The individual parts of his body matched up well with one another, that had always been an advantage in the water. Front crawl for long and middle distance, but he was equally effective swimming breaststroke. Anatomically ideal. He could breathe on both sides, which would allow him to keep either to the left or the right of the *Henry*; the body of the ship would at least cushion him from the worst of the wind and swell.

The woman at the checkout in front of Charles – white English calves, a floral skirt – packed a pink girls' frilly swimsuit along with a pink diving mask and snorkel into a plastic bag. A bottle of gin and three giant bags of crisps were already in it. He knew what Maude would whisper to him now: So very English indeed. So unhealthy! His wife would have said nasty things about Freda, too. This square human biscuit was English to the core. As was the beach: even the oldest of women spread out their blotchy-skinned, short-legged bodies on the rocks and opened and closed their pink, willing mouths like fish drowning in air.

Was he still missing Maude?

He didn't miss the tenth unwashed cup in the kitchen sink. Nor the cast-off t-shirts on the bathroom radiator that she meant to wear again and then forgot about. Never.

Just sometimes.

A while ago (thirteen months) he had occasionally smelled one of her t-shirts when he went to bed. Maude's body had changed once again in recent years, more in terms of how she looked overall than any specific physical change. It was evident in the daytime or in the morning light when she got dressed next to the bed. She seemed to be yielding more easily, her skin growing thinner. When she lay in his arms, always to the left, their bodies fitted together just as they always had. Of course, this was part of knowing each other so well, but that didn't explain it, right from the start their bones had accorded well, their limbs been the right length. That didn't disappear with age.

But sleeping together now was less often exciting and perhaps less exciting anyway. No more pheromones in an older body's odour, that's a chemical fact. For her. And for him? They went to bed separately on most of the evenings in the semester holidays when he was working from home. Maude was a night owl, he wasn't. She would play piano on the ground floor, two floors above he would fall asleep listening to her music.

He would look at her in the mornings. A sharp front profile, that curved nose with its wide nostrils. The bottom half of her face had softened with age. He wanted to press himself into her, feel her arms and shoulders, her breasts. It was almost shameful, how much he desired her after all these years. But only almost! He woke her up by kissing the patch behind her ear where her skin was stretched transparent-blue over the bone. Here was a path into her.

He felt more complete when he was with Maude, more full.

A wholerer man.

She was the person he shared countless memories with, who picked up on all his jokes. She was the centre of his family, all his contacts outside of work ran through her. She was his world beyond Chemistry.

Meanwhile he had to assume that on those evenings alone in the living room she hadn't only been playing the piano. She had been on the phone too.

When she arrived in the kitchen at noon in her dressing gown, he would have a second bowl of porridge with her. They would ring up Hazel, read each other items from the newspaper. The printed one, for the weekend. They shared the embarrassing things. That he liked After Eights. That she liked pink underwear (except on him) and would binge, at least once a month, on a whole season of some new series in a single day. Cumberbatch as Sherlock Holmes, today's London, he had to see it, those cheekbones, not to mention his deep voice. Charles pulled her up, she stretched out her bare feet, pushed them under his legs and threw a mandarin at him. He watched *Holmes* with her, fed her mandarin segments. But he didn't go on to accompany her through London; he went to his computer and worked. He imagined that these times would never end.

High tide was lapping over the bottom steps of the pier – stone, hewn for giants. Additional machines were springing into life in the arcade, one-armed bandits, air-hockey tables. You could test your reactions but needed an opponent.

A group of boys were catapulting themselves, one after the other, from the harbour wall into the water – directly next to the no-diving sign. His phone rang.

Charles' crossing had been registered, his arrival on land notified. The permission was valid, so Brendan said, from right now. A swimmer arriving with no paperwork whatsoever was allowed to stay on land in France for twenty minutes. That was the international law if you were shipwrecked. After that European law kicked in. From the twenty-first minute onwards, you counted as an illegal immigrant.

Take your passport at least to the boat.

The water in front of him was shimmering like thin steel. The route went with the tide, westwards out of Dover into the Channel, aiming for France's Cap Gris-Nez in a classic S shape that followed the push and pull of the water.

The task seemed to be the same for everyone. Except that the weaker you were, the further off course you were carried by the current. Someone like him would be dragged in an extra-large loop, drifting so much longer in the broth than a

32

younger person, becoming soft and puffy. No one managed a straight line.

He thought that was honest. True to life. If you are already at a disadvantage, you get dealt another blow.

You swam with supervision, safety measures, well prepared, everything humanly possible was done for you, you were fed, supported. You still had: the body and its needs. Breathing, the pull of the depths, the drift.

"See," his grandpa had said, "don't blink!"

Rule 8, in Charles' version of the Channel Crossing Association's guide: Don't think. Do it.

Rule 8, officially: There's no opponent in the water.

There is only you. It is not a game.

The machines were firing, tinkling, ringing.

But it was a game. Crossing was like tossing a coin. Just that you were the coin.

You flew, you soared up, you sank down.

The white-pink china figurine, a shepherd kneeling in front of a lady in hooped skirts, had been banished to the cupboard so that he could clear the table and spread out his maps. The wallpaper, soft red with a lime green stripe, was edged with roses. He had booked the B&B's first-floor room with sea view (from the side at least) months ago. Far below him, birds rocked on the waves, white and peaceful.

Rule 1: The Channel is not your friend.

He swore: boiling hot water was shooting out of the tap under the flowery porcelain mirror. Mixer taps were still deemed unnecessary in England. Burn or freeze, what else could he want? He shaved his calves, armpits and chest so that the protective grease would absorb better. His legs looked about thirty years old. Toes twenty. Arms forty-five. Occasionally he was surprised by the wrinkles between his nose and his mouth, as if they were something new. Inwardly he felt like he was living through all ages at the same time, seven and twenty-two and forty-one. Fell down the stairs with a baby in his arms; jumped from a rock on Sylt Island into the North Sea; hugged Silas after Camden Swimming Club's first victory in the relay. A staggering percentage of Channel swimming enthusiasts were over sixty. That was the age when you had enough money to prepare properly, the time to do it. Not so much a matter of strength as toughness. Success depended not only on your body, but on your determination, your preparation, your mind.

It was not a sport.

The folks on the beach called it a – challenge.

He had taken to saying that too.

With him following in tow, they would head out to sea. The cliffs almost transparent in the dawn light, slits just starting to show in the grainy blue-grey sky to the southeast. Brendan would decide if Charles' attempt was to take place. Last-minute updates, weather checks on www.windy.com.

In tow. That's what it would look like. In reality, there would be nothing connecting them at all.

If you didn't answer the pilot or even just trod water, the crew would pull you out. You gave up the right to make your own decision. The right to fight it.

When did a future collapse?

When was your wish definitively disregarded?

He had trained. And trained.

Shivered, sworn.

Sought a coach, put on a stone = ordered a whole load of Swiss chocolate online. Since Brexit, the British Toblerone was one triangle shorter than on the other side of the watery divide, and more expensive to boot. Sometimes he had spent the night in Portland Terrace, but only when the house was empty. He had spoken with Maude on the phone, even had the odd chat with her in their basement kitchen about everyday stuff. When it came to practical matters they had always worked well together, as parents too. She wanted something from him, but he didn't understand what. So, Silas had read the November letter. And, according to Maude, simply shaken his head. He, Charles, could sort that one out. "You owe it to him. Wasn't he your best friend?"

But that's not why she had clamped the letter to the fridge. Or it was only a secondary consideration. Primarily … well … yes, she wanted to remind him. Did he really not know why? And of what?

Slow as a snail he had crawled into the Isis in autumn to get used to the cold-water temperatures. The Isis was the name of the Thames in Oxford, which in turn was so called because even the oxen had shaken so much on fording the river here that their knees gave way. "Icy" was an understatement. In the shade of St John's boathouse, he would dry himself off after fifteen minutes, thirty minutes, an hour, pull on his thermals and his fleece layers. Then he would sit on one of the park benches in Christ Church Meadow. The frost-covered trees stood tall against the morning sky like mighty chunks of feldspar. Noiselessly crows snapped their beaks open and shut. They were watching over the bare branches, the warmth, time itself.

Smoke was coming from the chimney in the Shakespeare Inn, as if the low building had been issued straight from an eighteenth-century painting. What kind of cooking was going on here? Or was it really that dark and damp inside? The placard on the wall said 1642. Charles understood: English stonework. On the canal. Constantly exposed to the wind. They needed to check, In the middle of August, whether the chimney was drawing properly. The man on the terrace with a sun umbrella growing out of his table waved to him.

Charles shook Brendan's hand. His pilot, whose main job was a fisherman, preferred to be out and about at night. The sea chart in front of him glistened with salt. Brendan had fished even as a child. Family business. Who would have thought such a thing still existed? Now, in the summertime, he fished for people, pulled them alive from the sea.

He didn't have any children.

But there was another family member who would accompany them, Cedric. He wasn't up to much else.

"Sounds reassuring," said Charles.

Brendan laughed, something he could do as if in slow motion. Cedric had trained as a nurse. Don't worry. So had he.

Charles gave a dismissive wave. Did he really need to know everything? So, they would be starting at dawn. The moon had been on the wane for three days, calming the tides. If Charles needed more than seventeen hours, it would turn into a night-time adventure either way.

The rules followed Webb's first Channel crossing. On this landmass, 1875 was still recent. People lived in houses that had been built then. They were modest in their needs. Sunlit patches layered the sky like old jewellery, tarnished and chiselled by celestial hammers. A waitress, barely five foot tall, wiped the bird droppings from the tables. It was five o'clock, time to start serving again. The air smelled of seaweed. Waves of wind ran over the lawn, the pub sign, aquamarine-yellow and with Shakespeare's head on it, swung back and forth.

"Apple juice," said Charles.

Six hours at the latest before the start Brendan would give him a ring. The journey back from France was on the *Henry*. Three hours, four, depending on the swell.

He saw himself stretched out, a sleeping figure on the deck, wrapped in blankets. An ice grey beard in the first rays of sunshine.

"Ah, what're you on?!" said his pilot. He put his charges in the cabin. Upright, awake. "To check whether they're alright."

Brendan drank a pint of ale, set aside his glass, whacked Charles' final piece of homework on the table: the names of everyone over the last decades who had paid for their attempt with their life. "Sorry, fella." It had to be done.

It would strengthen his resolve.

Cables were strung over the road to the next pylon, where they were looped and hooked together to form a new night-sky constellation. The air was rustling, whistling, rubbing.

8 September 1954: Edward J. May. Alone. Corpse found in October off the coast of the Netherlands.

Summer 1984, Kumar Ananadan from Sri Lanka.

...

14 July 2013, Susan Maylor, a mile off France, circulatory collapse.

Nick Thomas, 45 years old, less than a mile from his destination, 27 August 2016. Sixteen hours in the water, heart attack.

Douglas Waymark, mid-forties, 8 August 2017, heart attack after the first S-bend in the middle of the waterway.

So did he see?

The last mile was the most dangerous. Rule 10: There is no certainty.

Charles swallowed the sweet juice.

Near the sea, water and grass merged. The blades ran in waves. Even the birds' wings took up the beat.

"It's a love-hate relationship," said his navigator. Short, fat arms, reddish eyelashes, t-shirt in bold yellow. A shirt for making landfall, he realised that now. You could see it when you were wading back from French sand towards the boat.

Brendan was wearing it for him. A shirt of hope.

The disappointments were shite. Sure, you had to reckon with them. A mighty challenge, from start to finish.

In silence they sat next to a hedge of dark sweet peas in full bloom. The first wasps buzzed around the blossoms, the beer and juice attracting them. The pilot hit out at one, missed it.

He would have to give himself over, said Brendan.

To whom?

The Oxford neighbours had stood in wellington boots in their garden, year in, year out; unlike Charles, they readily planted themselves in the soil. It was soft here. English ground was a kind of water that just about made it into a solid aggregate form. How long ago was Shakespeare? Every toddler here dreamed of fossils and mucked about in the earth. Being obsessed with the past had a different meaning in England than east of the River Rhine.

Charles handed the cheque for the final instalment across the table. He wanted to cross. The captain didn't want any dead customers. Damaging for business and sleep. Or the other way round, said the man in the landfall shirt and clipped the payment into a cheap folder. Floral pattern, faded.

Give yourself over.

"To you?"

"That too," said the pilot.

It was up to the adventurer to understand the meaning of his pact. "Distractions:" Storm, tankers, panic attacks, cramps without end.

The adventurer had settled his last debt, taken his cue from the seals and fattened himself up against the cold.

The adventurer liked his pilot. Hopefully the reverse was equally true. Fluffy seeds were blowing over the meadow, every evening you could see bunnies on the hop.

And what motivated Brendan? He needed the money. There wasn't much left in fishing anymore. Taking on the crossings was an obvious alternative. Charles assumed that he also enjoyed it.

He signed the agreement: he would comply.

To his surprise, he found himself sitting in a mill of light. There he was, on a bench in the Shakespeare Inn, under a squeaky Shakespeare sign, a shower of grains of light being ground down upon him. Hundreds of sacks of light-flour had exploded. A world without shade, glittering and dense. He had fallen into it fully upright.

Time that had missed its cue to run forwards didn't just turn around and run backwards.

Abigail was standing next to the bench he was sitting on and smiling at him.

Abigail, of all people.

"Oh, you again!" said a voice from behind him.

He turned around.

"You're up tomorrow!"

Her fuzzy hair reminded him of the prophetic old woman in the *Matrix* films. Didn't she bake biscuits for Neo?

"Oh darling," said Freda, "he really is more handsome than you." He should go right ahead and eat those biscuits tonight. Ginger, from the supermarket.

He tried to dispatch her with a small bow. How was she to know that he was swimming tomorrow? And he knew nothing?

Brendan had left the pub early, Charles had stayed on to order a Spaghetti Bolognese. It was a dead weight in his stomach now along with the chips, the last thing he needed was a story from Freda on top of it (= the Japanese man who paddled around in a circle like a goldfish; the drunk Frenchman who, when the ferry had hardly left Calais, jumped over board to swim back to France but got the coasts mixed up and went the whole way to England; John from New Zealand, who every year lasted exactly five hours in the water and then gave up). He had spoken with John just yesterday, on the Swimmers' Beach; it was his thirteenth trip from Australia.

She licked her lips, the metal parts of her weatherproof clothing jangling as if Freda herself were a Turkish crescent. And perhaps tonight was the last time in his life that he would go to bed.

"Bunny, you need a scheme."

A scheme, that sounded sensible. She dictated, he typed it into his calendar. Now that he wasn't looking at Freda, just listening to her, he liked her voice.

7:00 p.m. Go to bed (immediately)

2:30 a.m. Get up, stretch, shave

2:45 a.m. Breakfast (energy bar, tea)

3:15 a.m. Depart (order two taxis, one will come for sure)

3:30 a.m. Board boat

3:50 a.m. Leave Dover (estimate)

4:05 a.m. Arrive at Samphire Hoe

4:15 a.m. Swim to the beach

4:20 a.m. Arrive at beach

4:23 a.m. Last prayers (if you believed in that sort of thing, obviously; if you didn't, then just to be on the safe side)

4:30 a.m. Start

Out of excitement and perhaps a touch of superstition he pressed a goodbye kiss to her cheek. That he did this surprised him. The cheek felt real, that surprised him too.

She stroked his: "We'll meet again." Pause. Unusually, she wasn't smoking. He felt her watching him leave.

His phone showed fifteen degrees, but it felt like ten at most. Dry leaves whirled in the air, bare, almost wintery patches of ground shone next to spring-green street lights, as if a landscape always played through all seasons at once, fluid under the crust, everything else a cover, a trick of "nature" put on for man who, too focused on his immediate life, failed to see this grander picture speeding past.

Instead of sleeping, Charles walked around outside. A streetlamp, an electricity mast, a pub-sign in the wind. Hardly had he lain down and turned off the light before he saw Maude. To the left of her parting, her hair protruded by a fingertip. Maude's cowlick. He loved this spot. It was like a note. If he placed a finger on it, he could hear Maude's music. That was how it had always been. Crazy, really. Why should a cowlick on a girl's forehead, where the skin's smooth pores give way to hair, set you all a-flutter? But that is what had happened. With Maude. And with her sister Abigail.

The light was failing fast. Bushes were hanging from the cliff's selvedge, this monster bird plunged from the sky thousands of years ago, its body splatted out wide on impact down below, its wings erect, frozen.

Or a melted cloud after all? A transitory species straining to make its way back off land and into the salty water?

Iron-hard plant roots, grown out of nothing, grasped taut across the cracks in the stone.

In front of this stretched the Channel, a slab, grey-black as slate, and with a subtle glitter. Almost on the horizon, a container ship was moving eastwards; a boat as well as a mid-sized cargo ship were sailing in the English stretch. Lights;

not a soul to be seen far and wide. Just him. He took his finger off the app, the weather display disappeared.

Border control officers on either side observed every movement. Error prone. Technology observed every movement. The officers observed the machine read-outs. A lull? Traffic? One person staring at another person staring. Who was using which route, lightening which load of wood, metal, plastic, oil, or flesh and blood.

A mental process, Brendan had said. *It's your mind that decides.* The pilot saw the state of the candidates on the beach at the start, pale bodies peeling away from the shadows thrown by the cliffs, rubbing on more grease, jumping up and down with nerves. You couldn't see the tingling nerves in people's faces, the owner of the *Henry* had explained, because stress set the face like a mask. In their minds they had already been swimming for hours.

The tide, the moon, your mind.

Charles strolled in the direction of Samphire Hoe. Gulls shrieked, near the car park a horde of kids ran boisterously over the gravel; it was a long summer evening, and no one was sending them to bed. High-pitched voices, air like glass. Two men, barefoot and in grey shorts – he thought they must be a couple, so deliberately did they match each other – looked quietly out to sea. Shots of spray flared up intermittently.

Nobody else paid any attention to the man emerging from the waves further down the beach. His body was silhouetted against the silver horizon, the water splashed around his feet. He took off his goggles, picked a pebble from the ground – did everyone at the seaside reach for the same few gestures? –

and threw it in the air. The projectile traced a proud arc, hanging at its zenith like a lost celestial body. Its gaunt thrower turned on the spot and jogged off in the opposite direction, light-footed, long-legged, fast becoming a kind of insect. His back shimmered, as if a paper-thin, silver foil were growing from his shoulders; it must be the water rolling off.

By the sea, figures were magnified. Charles had reached the kiosks. An approach road had been cut through the rock, an information centre built, benches installed. Pennants flapped on the new piece of land that the excavations for the Eurotunnel had yielded. The vast car park stood empty, apart from two vehicles stationed at quite some distance from one another. In the dark pink of dusk, crows strutted over the "Meadowland" environmental project. He presumed they were searching for clothes hangers.

"Sea," he heard his grandpa saying, his father's father, "look, the sea. Swim!"

Grandpa had brought him to the North Sea, to a swarm of blue, before Charles' world entertained the difference between animal and wave.

"You see?"

Something underneath him had moved, had flown up, buzzed around his head. Gone. Back again. Light, spinning towards him like a rotating reel of thread –

"Blue!"

Grandpa with his soft, eastern European face next to him in the water, his blue eyes level with Charles', holding him by the chin.

Water!

Charles, two years old, moved through the foreign element with a fearlessness that would have taught anyone other than Grandpa what fear was.

"Sea!" said Grandpa and pointed out into the blue, and Charles understood that seeing and the sea were one.

He needed to go out just one more time, shortly before midnight. The water was deep blue with a few brighter strips; to the right of the cliffs, it swelled with a glittering dark yellow from the light of the buttery moon.

It was as if the Channel at this hour had neither desire nor strength. The wind had died down, as Brendan had forecast. The sea presented like a velvet dress of midnight blue, spread out on a sofa, deceptively soft.

Presence. Powerful, radiating.

Extension.

Victory. Self-possessed, beyond doubt.

Cool, night air blew from the ridges along the cliffs and their white footpaths. Sea-land, grass-sea, land-sea. Four times in February the ferry had missed the entrance to Dover port; the combination of current and the wind had pushed the heavy ship so strongly out of the navigation channel that all steering had been futile.

In the water there would be no opponent. Only exhaustion and exhilaration, temptation and strength.

That life was born of sauce, of energy from the sun in a puddle of H_2O, of chance, coagulation and x, was wondrous and remained so. Amphibian adventurers, loony creatures had crawled onto land, gasped for breath, panted, shaken themselves, immediately scrunched up their bulging eyes, blinded by the air's density of rays.

How did you know you had passed a threshold? What determined a catastrophe, a moment of realisation, a glance through a doorway or a snatch at a letter? Nothing actually changed; the collapse happened noiselessly, in your head.

In the narrow building in Kingston Road, his Oxford pad, he had re-read in his own time the letter that he had put in his jacket pocket in the kitchen in London. It wasn't about the lie, Maude had said.

He was ashamed, nevertheless. He had forgotten about this sheet of paper. Back then he had sown the seeds of discord.

And now? He read it again.

Dearest Maude,

How are you? My thoughts are with you, I am torn. I have had barely any contact with either Silas or you, and yet even from afar I can feel you pitying me. That's the worst thing of all!

You know how it is with me. In my heart of hearts, I never wanted anyone else but you. I can no longer watch you building your life, a life with Silas, on a lie. I have spent months wrangling with myself, but now I am writing to you.

Abigail and I had an argument a few days before the accident. I was woken up by the bedroom light being turned on in the middle of the night. She was standing in the doorway, drunk, naked under Silas' dressing gown, half undone.

She said she loved me. At the same time, she claimed to feel the same as you about Silas. To love him too. And yes, unlike her dear sister, she happened to love us both. "While you," she said to me, "are with me but carry Maude's photo in your wallet!" So, she, Abbie, had had enough. She had just gone to bed with Silas.

On that day, you had met up with a friend from school. I think you were planning on having dinner together. Do you remember that? Of course you do. How could any of us have forgotten those days on Sylt? But to you, to you at least, I can write openly. The way those days ended put everything into sharp relief. How blind we had been! We had to deal with things that just a few hours earlier we didn't even know existed.

Silas, said Abbie, had been amazing. So charming. Was I finally jealous now? Or horrified? And she kept jabbing me in the stomach with her finger – she was drunk, toppled over onto her side, curled up into a ball in the middle of our bed, still wearing Silas' dressing gown, and fell asleep.

The next morning, she avoided me. She appeared in good spirits, told us that she had to study for her teacher training exams, disappeared for hours at a time.

That was how things were until the accident. It changed us all.

I suppose you knew about the baby. Abbie was pregnant. She said it was mine. Now I am no longer sure. She implied she had been having an affair for a while. With Silas, presumably?

Why she did it – I cannot say. Was she angry at you? Because you were prettier, always first choice? At me? Or because life as a foursome, something that had seemed so simple, was no longer simple at all?

Because we had to make some decisions now that a baby was on the way. Whose father was unclear.

Did Silas ever tell you any of this? I don't mean to insinuate anything. Maybe he didn't know. About the pregnancy, I mean.

Maude: this letter is for you. I want you to be free to build the life you want, without any lies. Silas – and her. I had to tell you.

If you need me, Maude: I am here for you.

And will be, whatever happens.

Forever yours,

Charles

2

Charles looked out to sea, into the wind. The expanse in front of him was dark and flat, only the two port entry lights rippled their reflection across the water. The deck was swaying slowly, he swayed with it. Brendan had clipped ridiculous orange light sticks onto the back of his swimming trunks. He could see them flashing, and now he too was casting a reflection.

Forwards, stroke by stroke. *Never give in to drowning. It's cold and makes you shiver*. The *Henry* chugged along, leaving eddies of oil-slicked water in its wake.

Mister C? Do you listen at all!

The night ferry to Dunkirk had left, the one from Calais was still miles away. Cedric, the other man on the *Henry*, was at the wheel. Hour after hour Charles would hear the engine, its screw blades churning.

He was an idiot.

The idiot smiled at Brendan, who was slipping on a pink rubber glove with practised ease. "You'll become an honourable fish."

An honourable fish! The grease protected his skin but did nothing for the cold. It would be at least forty thousand strokes. That chafed. Lumps of the stuff clung to his neck, his shoulders, under his chin. Some relief. The wind buffeted noises around Charles' head, like a child shovelling sand.

Cedric – stocky, muscular, no tattoos (too chicken?, too expensive?, the wrong clichés in Charles' head?) and with a pleasant face, the metal rings in his nose and bottom lip notwithstanding, -- Cedric had written the registration number on his upper arm back at the jetty with indelible marker. In pink. The chap had enjoyed that. The night air was cold.

Charles pulled his mouth sharply to the left, to the right, spreading the protection into the last folds of skin.

Thankfully no one besides the fisherman and his crew could see him now. The Channel Swimming Association cheerily dispensed well-meaning advice to all interested parties on their website: really better to not bring loved ones along. You might slip into states you would prefer your nearest and dearest not to see.

A smart tip on a commercial site. He knew what it was really saying. Did the platform owners know it too? Love cannot survive all odds.

Idiot.

Samphire Hoe, from the front this time. Was that the wind pounding in his ears now? Or panic? Did everyone hear this howling? No, in his mind he hadn't been bravely striking out for hours on the open sea; he was a mouse, retreating desperately inside himself and hoping to disappear for good.

Charles the reluctant Houdini. People like him (= slow) started at the western end of the artificial finger of land to avoid any danger of the tide pulling them back into Dover harbour. In the past, you would have dropped into the Channel from the town's sea wall, a dramatic iron accordion structure over which streams of rust tumbled wildly, or swung your way down a peeling ladder, a white slug against the reedy green and red-gold hues of the metal that some days also shimmered with oil. Underfoot, narrow concrete spurs jutted out; in the photos they lay across the water like ivory piano keys.

These days, you picked your way over large pebbles, seaweed and rubbish lying between the wall and the nudist beach to start the ultimate test. No drop, just a simple, banal walk.

Could your actions turn out smarter than you yourself thought?

That's what Charles was hoping.

With a heavy suck, Brendan pulled the glove from his fingers. Matilda, a recently retired primary school headteacher, the last to jump on board before they left (= slow), straw-blonde hair, an oversize pair of sunglasses on a gold chain over her ample bosom, clamped a piece of paper onto a board. Mealtimes, changes in the weather, what section was reached when, she recorded it all. Her handshake had been limp. Who where when why how long with what to what end.

Those were the column headings. Freehand, the teacher drew perfectly straight lines between them. Charles would have bet money that this woman, appointed official observer of his crossing, would write legibly even in gale-force ten. Nobody mentioned that she was there for insurance purposes. In case Charles died, every decision made on the boat had to be documented. His life insurance would go to Maude. He didn't know whether endangering your life was covered, or whether crossing a narrow strait counted as endangering your life. Nor did he give a bloody damn.

4:10 a.m., arrival at Samphire Hoe, bow facing southwest. In addition to the headlights, Brendan switched on the *Henry*'s fog beam. Starring: her majesty, the beach. Noiselessly stretching herself right up to the foot of the cliffs in the flare of the electric rays. Lying there like a bridal train of seaweed, pebbles and sand. Only the bride was missing. The *Henry* floated a hundred yards off the coast, the closest she could get to land.

"Jump," shouted Brendan, "now!"

After the first hour he had settled. Head down, stroke, stroke, stroke etc. Up on six. Breathe. For every stroke, a word: now, go, push. Monosyllabic, no let-up. When he heard another voice at some point, and it was at some point, because time became fluid when what counted as forwards could only be determined by a ship's bow, at some point he heard a voice that wasn't his own and turned over onto his back. He saw the sky.

"Feed!"

"Everyone swims in a wobbly line to start with," said Brendan, "never mind!"

It grew light. Purple-grey bellies, faintly golden cheeks. Obediently he slipped back onto his stomach. Next to him a shining white spot the size of a lifebuoy bobbed on the calm waves. It was so light by now that the sun was admiring itself in the water. His stroke rate, which had fallen by the end of the first hour to twenty-six, had shot back up to thirty after a hundred and ten minutes in the water.

Two hours in.

"Feed."

Freestyle, Charles swam a mile of front crawl in thirty-one minutes. His pilot had agreed to some breaststroke in-between, as long as he stuck to the schedule, followed his own rhythm. The succession of movements should be like a regular pulse. Horrible noradrenaline and sweet endorphins coursed through his veins. The blond patches of morning where his hands churned the water turned rusty red like fish blood. Cedric and Matilda stood at the railing, their faces dappled with gold, and held an extra-large whiteboard over the side of the boat. For years, Hazel had hoarded exactly the same board in her room like a secret, smooth-skinned, animal. They had drawn a ferry on it, huge. The cliffs glistened behind them, Dover lay safely in its nest over four miles away, swimmers were getting ready for their morning training. He was out at sea, he was on his way.

Cedric screwed up his eyes. Matilda was blinding him as much as the candidate's black swimming hat. Used to be a teacher, the pink skirt and pink shawl a nasty disguise. He grinned. He had already seen off a few of her kind, shot their nerves. Time would tell whether this one here could hack it. 'Cause it was the sea. Was family. And relaxing: no girl-friends, no pug. Always a swell, no one could tell if you were a bit loose around the ol' joints. Never mind an effin' fidget! Cedric, stay put. He whistled to himself and watched their candidate. Quite a kicker, this one. Flogging himself down there in the wet and not one bit better than Cedric. Just less dough than before the crossing. People like Mister C were all trying to find or lose themselves or prove something to someone by swimming to France. Chrissakes! What was the point of it? Of course, he could have put them right before they had splashed the cash. Had they asked. But they didn't ask. And he wouldn't have told them. It was too nice here for that: a little bit of casual steering, marking the route, snoozing on deck. He phoned Helen when he fancied. If he didn't fancy it, what could he do about the sea? Swallowed all the signal again.

Mod-est, thought Charles, mea-sure. He had changed his pool swimmer's kick to require less footwork. In the sea you lifted a layer of living water, could let your face drop down on the return, relax your neck. Control, no fear.

Com-mit- – the ground was pretty shallow here – ment-self-be-lief. About 150 feet deep on average, going down to a rough, wildly undulating, almost mountainous bottom, once home to mammoths and lions. Red deer had roamed the tropical forest, in the stone age people had fashioned arrowheads from the forks and crowns of their antlers, rhinoceroses had trampled the earth. Probably sunk by a tsunami around 6200 BCE. Until then, the British Isles had been visibly attached to the Continent. Man and animal had crossed back and forth with dry feet. Centuries of grief must have passed as the rising sea levels turned the homelands between East Anglia, the Netherlands and Northern Germany into an archipelago.

And so he paddles over fossils, over primeval, half tropical foliage, over stone age axes, petrified sets of antlers that branch out like giant spoons, over long-scattered needs, dreams and souls.

De-di-ca-tion. Two by two, a long stroke. Effortlessly, his body was gliding after his arms, and so things went for a while, almost pleasant, and then suddenly his right arm scooped into something soapy. The first jelly fish, this early? The thing he touches, without managing to keep a hold of it, is sticky. He lets go of it, but it doesn't let go of him. In a panic, he strikes out to the side, comes up.

He has caught the end of the rod dangling the little pack of carbohydrates his way. He is tangled up in the line. His own plastic bag. How stupid!

Fortunately, Matilda is preoccupied with rolling up her sleeves. He sends a gasp of thanks to the makers of slippery polyester blouses. Only now does he realize, they are feeding him? So another hour has passed?

Cold, wet, Charles. How he had stood (= only just now) on the pebbles of Samphire Hoe, illuminated by the *Henry*, at one with the scenery (= he thought), and yet sticking right out of it (= he felt), alone like never before. He had stared at the *Henry*. The cliffs behind him were bursting with their own strength. Another minute, his pilot had called, an astonishingly long, black line at the railing. And for one whole minute, the beach in front of Charles had made space for something to happen that he hadn't yet really begun to comprehend, even though that person standing there was the driving force behind it all. He had jumped up and down, lost all sensation.

"Give me my bottle," he called up the side of the boat.

From now on he only wanted to drink from his old green bottle, tied to a rope and flung down to him.

In truth – he wanted to vomit.

Seasick wasn't the word for it. The sea was rolling, he was rolling with the sea and rolled himself even further onto his side, the only way to breathe air not water – and the wind would grab the sea that was already rolling and roll it again, while the boat's screw churned up any remaining order in the ocean. Apparently there were people whose sense of balance coped just fine with this kind of multi-directional, roiling spray of reality. He was not one of them.

He spat out the last mouthful of gel. Matilda, pink face, yellow hair, yellow necktie, gave him a thumbs up. That was the sign language here. He had seen more raised thumbs on this day than throughout the rest of his life. Brendan was steering, Cedric was sleeping. They were reckoning with a night swim.

Part of Charles' brain accepted that he was no longer sure whether this was the start of the third or the fourth hour, another part turned his body back into its swimming position.

To France? Oh no, he wasn't swimming there. He was cleverer than that. He was swimming from feed to feed. "You," he had overheard Freda at the training beach telling Mandy, a woman due to start in the same tidal window as him, "you swim until your tits are dragging over French ground."

Mandy, mother of two, had turned red.

Shi… seawater already slugged. *Don't laugh, Charles!*

The tide, the moon, your mind. Breathe out underwater, mouth closed. On the sixth stroke, eyes and lips open. He kept to the right of the *Henry*. Saw – when he saw anything – the open sea. Well, nearly. He saw the Channel.

In his B&B they were serving the English breakfast now. The thought of it already seemed to come from a drowned world. After – was-it-three-hours? – in the icy salt-soup he may well have gone a bit daft. In the left frontal lobe of his brain, control and doubt were out for the count, on the right perseverance and strength were circling each other, happily self-absorbed.

Last week he had found a Playmobil figurine on the beach, a ranger with splayed legs planted on a patch of green, his arm up, as if waving to an invisible central command. The green and brown colours in his suit had been almost entirely washed away by the salt water, the helmet splintered in part. Charles had cleaned the tiny head piece and placed the submerged guardian of the land on his bathroom windowsill. Burning light pierced the figurine from all sides.

He felt like the ranger was sitting on his skull.

The sun was meanwhile so high above him that the water flowing over his bare back no longer blocked its warmth. He was glad he had mixed sun cream into the Vaseline that the skipper had rubbed onto him. Roll-over, the next slug of water. And if he puked now? After thirteen, or seventeen, or x hours in the mucky broth his face would look bigger than at the start. Bigger was a euphemism. If you weren't careful, even your tongue swelled up to twice its size. Then the puke couldn't get out.

He swam and swam, and nothing changed. The water kept on carrying him, the water kept on pushing him back, the water kept on contradicting itself and only giving the impression of carrying. It lied, it gnawed, it weighed down on him. In this respect, it was like Maude.

Single rhythm: swim, swim, swim.

Swim-ming, two beats.

Well, well, well.

Well, hell, swell.

Looking up to his left on a breath, he could see the guillotine smoothness of the *Henry*'s side lifting itself up out of the water on every sixth syllable. Nothing else happened.

The captain's deck was full of instruments for measuring things; they resembled egg boxes for a battery of crazy Easter bunnies or a dentist's forceps for enormous teeth. Minute by minute, the correct route was traced on top of his actual one. The red lifeboat in the stern swang on its hook from left to right and back again.

Nothing else happened.

He was an idiot. A contented idiot. Swim, swam, swum. Sick as a dog, green at the gills. All the brochures tell you: your body starts burning fat. Accurate rubbish. His body had started eating his bones, his tendons, his nerves. His body was eating itself up.

So something was happening after all.

And then nothing happened for another while.

His legs had gone. The arms were still there.

So was the glass half empty or half full? The Channel was full. And his glass of life? Even if the wrong side of sixty could hardly count as 'half' any more.

Tick, tack, tock.

The answer came to him in a flash. The glass was half full. What else! Half full, with emptiness.

He closed his eyes to breathe. Opened them under water. Any pair of goggles would give in to the water eventually. It was smart to ration sight from the start.

Soft needles of light danced around him. The Channel was hanging in the balance, content to float inside itself. So wasn't it nice of him, Charles, to join in? The particles drifting through the water were his excretions, his warmth, his steam, his drive.

A piece of Charles.

Otherwise, nothing happened again for a long time.

Brendan was standing at the railing, the sun lit up his curls from behind, they were almost as white as the ship's skirts.

Feeds on the half hour from now on!

Charles had done four hours.

Chocolate, if he wanted it.

He did.

Lifted his head, sucked. His body hung diagonally in the water, bait on an invisible line. He was feeding his liver, his heart.

On crackling rays he struck onwards, into the waves.

He was lying flat on his back. Something tickled his nose and slowly he climbed out of a red-gold syrup of exhaustion and sun, back into a world full of voices. Over him, near enough to kiss, hovered a familiar face. It grinned.

Charles, on his towel at the side of a swimming pool on Sylt Island, jumped up. Or, he wanted to jump up, but actually only managed to wrench open his eyes.

Silas had approached the girl. From England, what's more – quite a coincidence! He wanted to introduce Charles to her. That he should also present the girl to Charles was logical. Nobody thought anything of it.

Only later did it seem poignant.

Silas said, "My best friend."

The girl said, "And that's Abigail, my sister."

Charles, either still half in his dreams or plunged back into them, turned his head. Yes, there really was another person there, between the water and dry land. Blonde, freckles on her nose, curious. At least that was the pose she struck.

"See you at the ice-cream parlour," said Silas and straightened up. So did the girls.

Charles blinked, taking in the entire length of the first English girl's legs, right up to her bikini bottom. It was blue. A stretch of bare belly. A red spaghetti-strap top, medium-sized chest. Abigail said, "Seems pretty lazy, your friend."

If it were true that everything is decided in the first three seconds, then it was all over already.

A tempting thought.

All the same, one thing was true: He had to thank Silas for Maude. Silas and, strictly speaking, Abigail. She had spotted the English lads at the pool days earlier, had convinced Maude to hang about on the bench by the diving tower. Until Silas finally did the decent thing (= what Abbie wanted: the boys should come over to the girls), she admitted as much after a few days. The men daring and self-assured, the ladies meekly waiting to be courted, those old roles.

And this in 1976? Exactly, said Abbie. England had its music. And Glastonbury. And its weed. And Portobello Road. It was fine if a few traditions were left untouched. Abbie was a Chemist, a trainee teacher. She liked how all the elements were ordered, the laws of nature immutable.

Otherwise, she was like her younger sister. That's what everyone said. And everyone meant something different by it. Charles thought that nature had practised for the second on the first. Maude said it was a cheek even to think such a thing, let alone go and say it. Abbie was insulted when she heard, insulted straight out, and then again, later that evening, when she privately pondered Charles' words in the bathroom and found herself thinking: damned nature. By this, she was less concerned with the equation of genes = the past, as with her heart = right now. Only Silas thought nothing at all. Charles' concern with what Silas might be thinking disappeared. He didn't even notice himself not noticing. He simply forgot about it, looked into those big, light brown Maude-eyes, those big, light blue Abigail-eyes, as if he were alone in the world with the girls, and disappeared in their gazes. The eyes were accompanied twice over by an equally large, pretty mouth in which he would also have liked to disappear, twice over. With Abbie, her forehead and chin were crowded out by her eyes and mouth. A shame, but pretty nevertheless. Abbie loved large floral-print dresses. Dresses that only women like. Men didn't notice these garments, not the same way they noticed shorts or spaghetti tops. Maude said Abbie was the quieter of the two of them. More intelligent in any case.

Two days after they had met, the four of them were sitting together in Westerland's most expensive restaurant and eating lobster, thanks to an unexpected gift from Silas' father, Tex. Charles could have raised his eyebrows at the things Silas shared with his father (met some girls, etc). Had he rung him up just to tell him? But in actual fact he didn't think anything of it, and Tex had probably given his son the money just like that, an advance for a special occasion. Silas put his arm around the back of Maude's chair and, less than an hour later on the path through the dunes, around Maude. Abbie, wearing Maude's spaghetti top and mini-skirt, told Charles, who was carefully keeping his arms to himself, that he would appear to have the emotional life of a teaspoon.

Was that being quiet? Not to mention intelligent?

"Teaspoons get hot," said Maude.

"Only if you stick them in the cup and let them stir," Abbie retorted.

They howled with laughter. Nothing would ever again match this kind of humour. They were just twenty and the world not one day older. It was vibrating.

They had been swimming in a blend of sugar, kisses and alcohol. Glasses half full? Half empty? They drank straight from the bottle, passed it round from mouth to mouth.

The four people in the dunes embraced, tried to go a few steps, stumbled, laughed. In the moonlight the sandy hills resembled disproportionate sea molluscs, their shells shimmering with a mother of pearl coating and sporting bizarre, snail-like outgrowths and moles that sprouted beards of grass. Even the sometimes too sensible, mannerly Maude was so full of red wine, lobster and hormones that she no longer cared how much sand was sticking to her hair or breasts. They had barely met, knew nothing about each other beyond what they were sharing and talking about now. There were no mutual friends, no preconceptions. This was happening for the first time in their lives, they gave it no further thought, just took it as a kind of freedom, a fuller existence in the here and now. What a coincidence they had met! A gift. And so things happened as they were meant to happen; they visited each other, took the bus to the south side of the island where the dunes were flatter, hairier, and the island tapered to a point. Once they even trudged out with a guide onto the mudflats, it looked harmless enough; between muscle shells, wormcasts and with the sun steaming down on them they wandered about. Inwardly they were waiting for the evening. It was their release, Maude brought along the music, Charles and Silas olives, cheese and wine, Abbie "the sticky stuff." The girls swapped around their clothes, they only had one pair of shorts and the same bikini tops, just in blue or red. The sun sank late and slowly, they called the music that they played their music for sinking away, Charles held Maude in one arm, Abbie sank into his other, Silas lay across them. Charles felt less on the Abbie-side, but he felt her all the same.

Because it wasn't true about the first three seconds. Because that was always a story cut short.

Steeply the ladder of the *Henry* soared up into the cradling air. Next to it swung a compass, a watch, a torch. They were hanging on a chain around Brendan's neck. Brendan's head and upper body too hung downwards, next to the ladder, leaning over to Charles. He had fallen behind schedule. But had recently regained his original stroke frequency. Almost.

Far above the end of the ladder the sun quivered in the sky.

Finally Charles could throw up. Come on, it was time for some credit here, wasn't he a bit of a champ: swimming and pissing at the same time, swimming and puking. Even if you weren't aiming for a record, speed was of the essence: think of that tide carrying everyone towards Calais where the heavy shipping makes it too dangerous to land, pulling you away from even the slightest outcrop of rock, anything that might count as land, anything you could touch, in order to finish some-time-tonight, be-finished-released-saved.

A mass of thickly glimmering blue shot down over Charles. He took his leave with a short nod, slipped back into his watery equilibrium. Swimming was like lying down now. For weeks his limbs had juddered asleep making swimming motions; in future, in even his deepest dreams he would hear the slap of the waves.

Blue, his grandpa had said.

See!

One by one they piled out of Tex's yellow Citroen, stretching their legs after the bumpy ride. Abbie and Silas emerged from the passenger side, Maude from behind the driver, and Charles, who had been sitting between the girls on the backseat, followed her.

1977, the summer after Sylt. Charles was studying Biochemistry in Oxford, Silas Economics in London, and Maude was at the Vienna Conservatory. Abbie, the only one earning a salary, was working in Reading as an assistant teacher. Charles had seen a lot of her. To his own surprise. Her porridge was deemed a wonder, she polished off two bowlfuls of it herself every morning, never with any fruit. Fruit was overrated, she had chemical proof of that. The rationale for the weekends turned out to be equally chemical, albeit in a different way. Charles had become immensely popular with the students sharing his staircase. Abbie could make stews, pies, lamb with mint sauce. She liked cooking to relax, prepared copious amounts of food and then gave it away. She sat on Charles' bed munching her breakfast and explained how her recipes worked. Who would have thought: it was all down to chemistry.

He really wasn't bothered.

"It all tastes good to me, dear."

Charles' friends were jealous. What a bird! She was up for anything? He was glad of her, he liked to say that. To them and to her. Abbie knew the story with him. There was no hiding it. She came to visit and told him about Maude. She seemed to understand his feelings for her sister. She stoked them further. He trusted her.

She ended up staying the night. He lay in his bed, she on a mattress on the floor next to it. She began staying more frequently. They lay in his bed. Or on the mattress. Sometimes they swapped over at noon. In Maude's absence, Abbie filled the void.

He barely met up with Silas at all that year, with Maude just once, in London, while Silas was there. Silas, who, as soon as he had some free time, headed off for Vienna. Train, ferry, train. Flying was expensive, the journey long.

In Maude's absence, Charles saw her by speaking with Abbie. And sleeping with her.

After Tex's clattery old banger, Levain was all the more impressive. A gravel drive, dwarf laurel trees, a French stone châtelet. It had style. The ground floor, the former servants' quarters, was given over to the laundry room and Tex's workshop, the kitchen was on the first floor, and this already commanded a sweeping view over the local mulberry and walnut plantations to the Cevennes. Tex had turned the entire second floor into a music room, where Maude could use the grand piano; bedrooms and bathrooms were located on the floor above. At the bottom of the garden full of lavender, roses and a giant magnolia, a stream gurgled. Damp like England, who would have thought it?

On Sylt, they had shared everything. Sylt had turned fluid with water, sun and wine. Hazy boundaries between arms, legs, breasts, although it hadn't gone beyond kissing and petting. He was sure never to have kissed Silas. But how could you be sure of anything when there were regularly a few hours of the night that were total blanks? Their time together now felt more orderly. Albeit not totally. The deviant sand of Sylt still rubbed between them, even the division of rooms (Silas and Maude on the fourth floor, Abbie and Charles below on the third) was based on it. In their first summer, both Silas and Maude had been seeing other people, Silas less so, as was always the case with Silas (= he never got as far as a relationship), Maude more so, but still nothing longer than three months. Both had ended these relationships, Silas wrote to Charles about it, and Maude had flown from Vienna to London to visit a couple of times; she spent every minute with him, wrote Silas. For Christmas, he sent Charles a packet of Austrian Mozartkugel chocolates. The two of them celebrated together in Vienna, Maude's parents didn't mind, after all Abbie had gone up to Newcastle to be with them (the dutiful daughter), and for a short time Charles was cross about this. He forgot about it by resolving to visit Maude in Vienna himself, but then, before he had managed to take this in hand, they were already clambering out of the car in Levain-le-Bain.

Maude was more beautiful than the previous year. Charles and she had written to one another over the intervening months, he loved composing letters, at least to her, she replied, and he had started picking up trinkets for her from places he visited: an almost perfectly heart-shaped stone on a path in the Cotswolds, the cast of a dinosaur's tooth from the Natural History Museum, which she, as she repeatedly told him, used in Vienna to spear Mozartkugels. She was no stranger to him as he sat squashed between the two in Tex's car, one sister to the left, the other to the right, their different scents met and mingled, for a few seconds they were one and the same, then they became distinct again, it was enough to make you dizzy. Charles closed his eyes and enjoyed the dizziness.

That these holidays were different wasn't down to Tex, or Levain, or that the sea was missing. It first and foremost had to do with Charles and Abigail. Abbie was a loyal soul. That sounded more trite than it was; it wasn't trite at all, in fact; his pleasure in her physical company had grown by the month. She was cheerful and excessive and commanded something that was foreign to him: the ability to invite, share, kick over the traces. She often wanted to do some exercise but ended up reading a book instead; she wanted to lose weight and then there she was, cooking again; she ate and drank too much and turned soft in his arms as the day turned to evening. Then she would curl up; he half expected to hear her purring and was touched by how childlike she appeared at times like these – it was as if the clever Chemist, quietly mocking him (she still sometimes called him a teaspoon) had been swallowed up for good.

Once a week they played squash on his college court. When Abbie chased Charles around the narrow hall, beating him, each of them working the other, they were one unit, one body nearly, and neither wouldn't have swapped with neither. Yes, that way round: a double negative. That was chemically correct. All-important bonds were drawn double. Charles was tough, tougher even than Silas, that was the only reason he had won the bet about who could jump fastest fifteen times in a row from the tower into the Westerland swimming pool; Abbie's reactions were more self-assured. She moved in with Charles for the holidays. This wasn't allowed, but his room was big enough for the two of them. A desk against the wall, a built-in wardrobe, a narrow bed in the corner. The kitchen, shower and toilets were shared along the corridor. A beige bench ran in front of the two wide, floor-length windows and around the corner, looking out over the wall to the college gardens. Waving tree-tops, moving skies. With Abbie you could share the silence. They halved the biscuits that Charles' mother sent, sometimes he invited his girlfriend to the cinema: Agatha Christie, or *Saturday Night Fever,* and then *Star Wars*. They saw Buñuel's *Obscure Object of Desire* twice so that he, Charles, could learn something about the battle between the sexes. But he didn't learn anything. Abbie now wore fewer florals more black or blue, a tight grey skirt, a stretchy top. Sexually, she had seemed more experienced than him, he didn't want to know why and in any case they were more or less equal now in the experience stakes. She was easy to sleep with, the half-feminist, as she called herself. More women in science! Blue stockings? Absolutely. With a seam. Romantic, solid. She didn't take the pill (a chemical bomb, her body belonged to her), so they used condoms and Charles was happy with that, he didn't know anything else. Abbie enjoyed shaking things up a bit, sometimes wanted it straight – after squash, for example, without a shower. Sweat and filth were all part of being human, she liked to say, they were all elements = building blocks of life.

It was a physical thing.

And he didn't just mean her with that, he meant himself too.

And Maude.

She knew about his relationship with Abbie. How could she not have done? Silas as well. Abbie was helping Charles find his way, that's what he told himself. Loosen up, have more friends, quit being so shy. All the same, he was enough of a realist also privately to admit that these were pleasing delusions on his part. One thing, however, certainly was real: when he was with Abbie he managed to forget he was jealous of Silas.

Even better: not be jealous in the first place. Silas was his best friend.

And Maude: wasn't her first love music?

It was too complicated.

And his studies were full-on. But things were working out, were working out really quite well. At the college summer ball they danced, boozed, danced. Well past midnight, he brought his girlfriend the x-th ale in the festival tent on the back quad, where at other times the ghosts of medieval scholars were reported to wander. On this night, Deep Purple, Rolling Stones and Zappa were thundering out of the speakers and a local band, Greenwood Great, were doing their best to shake up all the spectres and knock their bones together. They certainly achieved this with the living. Abbie was standing with Lawrence, the best-looking student from the Middle Common Room, amidst a group of Chemists. Lawrence, hopelessly drunk, was almost swooning at her feet. Had entwined his fingers in her curls. When Abbie noticed Charles, she seemed momentarily irritated – she, too, was well-oiled – then her eyes lit up, as if he were a marvel. It made him feel suddenly wanted on earth like never before. Marriage was in the air. Other couples were getting married. Their peers were constantly saying yes in the college chapel, you had to book six months in advance. And there was heavy competition: Lawrence & Co were willing and on the prowl day and night. For Charles there could be no question of anything of the sort. It wouldn't have been any different with Maude. He wasn't made for marriage, a mortgage, kids.

The other difference between their first and second summer, between Sylt and Levain, had to do with Silas and Maude. They showed photos of Viennese balls and concerts and looked like they had stepped out of a fairy tale. The snappy economics student, the impeccable pianist, simply made for one another. Silas had a golden aura, Maude a silver one, all the bets were on that they cut a *bella figura* in bed too. Stop, Charles, in the first place that was mean, second a taboo, and third Maude was already laughing at him: "there!"

In the photo that she had thrust under his nose, her hair was sticking up wildly and her mouth covered in chocolate. She was licking a half-bitten Mozartkugel, which she really had speared with the dinosaur's tooth. Behind her shoulder, he could see a shock of blonde hair. Definitely with a smeared gob too.

Maude, the tease. She gave him the picture to keep.

Ok, he demanded it.

When she handed it over, she wrote a dedication on it: For Charles, our sharpest tooth.

Very funny. Charles lay awake on his bed in the room underneath Silas and Maude. Maude practiced on the piano up there five hours a day. He listened to her; he could almost see her as she played, from the left, from the right, from behind. He didn't need x-ray eyes for that. Thanks to the way the rooms communicated through the wooden external walls and thin ceiling, it was as if he and Maude found themselves in one long ear canal. Charles was at the entrance, Maude was the ear drum, and the whole world trembled inside her piano. The very walls of the villa bound them together. He could feel Maude.

And he understood a part of her when he heard how she worked, corrected herself. He liked it. She too was tough.

Silas, a Leo through and through, slept a great deal. His finance studies in London were hard going. He only seemed semi attracted to Maude. Silas, the convinced anti-monogamist. Charles knew what he was like, after all. Abbie sat with Tex in the kitchen or strolled about the garden, advising on chemical fertilizers. Otherwise, Charles planned day trips with the car. Silas, Tex or Abbie had to drive, neither he nor Maude possessed a licence, and so he made sure they sat together on the back seat. Silas never objected, he was less attentive to Maude than his letters had given his friend in Oxford to believe. Charles told himself he was maybe just imagining it, and yet he wanted to whistle for joy. Whistling was about the extent of his musical abilities. He could whistle fragments of melodies, mostly children's songs, and imitate a few birds.

In the night-time the air smelled of sage. Cicadas sang. If you sat by candlelight on the veranda, you would see glow-worms climbing invisible ladders all around. Abbie had the relevant chemistry of light effects to hand; after a while, Maude whispered: "males are mad!"

Out of the dark came unexpected confirmation from their host, who was just heading out for a final inspection of the silkworms in his mulberry trees. Once again Charles was struck by Tex's similarity to Silas. Their voices had the same melodious ring. Perhaps the untimely death of Silas' mother had made them this close.

Maude was not for budging. Abbie looked questioningly over at Charles. When he gave no sign of moving either she stood up, smoothed down her skirt and went with Tex.

Charles found himself observing Tex more closely. The old guy would give the first cut of the roast to Maude. Then Abbie. He had noticed this for a while. He had noticed it because he hadn't liked what he was seeing. Tex gave Maude the first cut and Abbie the next, more succulent piece. Abbie got the first, hottest slice of toast. And to Abbie went the last, sweetest mouthful of homemade elderflower cordial.

Should he be jealous? If you had to ask yourself this, you weren't.

In the second week, Silas and Maude began to practice a couple of pieces together. Charles sat on the yellow chaise-longue in Tex's living room and listened. Silas' oboe rose and fell like a human voice, carried by the tones of the piano. He could sense his friend reaching out to Maude in the melody, how her musical phrases were searching for Silas. And yet then the dynamics would change once more, Maude avoid the oboe, hide.

She turned her head and winked at him.

Perhaps he, Charles, was part of the act? He was happy with that.

He had all the time in the world.

By the third week, he spent these afternoons mentally standing behind Maude and undressing her. He was so close to her that he could see the pattern of narrow blue veins where her skin was stretched almost transparent behind her ear, following the curve of the skull. He leaned over, smelled her, kissed Maude on that blue-tinged shadow, or less kissed her than breathed on her, consuming her with his eyes, nose and mouth. His other self, that new self that was spun from love, helplessness and diffidence, touched her as if she were the world's greatest treasure. Maude's dress gave way or came undone; and while Charles' hand reached over her shoulder to caress her arm, he also followed her right down on the inside, into her fingertips, and felt that even though in reality (which reality?) he was sitting on the sofa, she knew exactly what he was doing – and wanted. And she was enjoying it. He had hesitated because shortly after Sylt he had no longer been sure. Maude had declined to come to Oxford. They only wrote to each other, never visited. She belonged to Silas, he respected that – if even just for his friend's sake. But now it felt different, right. Silas was in the room too, a voice that wove through Maude and Charles' encounter, helped get things started, but otherwise had only a minor role to play, if any at all.

"Noon," Matilda called from the boat. True noon. This too they had learned from the pilot. Every day the sun traced a different arc; there was the chronometer's midday and local midday. Channels and currents changed almost hourly. No watch, no map could ever capture what was real, what was now.

True noon, thought Matilda, time to get undressed. Only the sky, the skipper and the nose ring-wannabe would see her eczema. By her watch it was shortly before one. She observed Cedric from the corner of her eyes as she stepped out of her skirt. The kind of boy who maltreated the school drum-set as a ten-year-old in a Spiderman costume and was such a fidget that he broke a window a week. Forty and no proper job, but a young girlfriend to make up for it. She had observed the two of them in the ice-cream parlour a few days ago. With a pug (the girlfriend). And a shiny collar (girlfriend and pug). The girl had greeted her. Clearly the women in the town were talking about her. Who's that, just moved here? Old bag! Nobody moved here anymore. She had returned the greeting. Pug-girl had to be the daughter of one of the other old bags.

True noon. A yawn struck across the firmament, sucking at the atmosphere. Brendan, lying on his back on deck, stared upwards. He never slept on his ship. He was too fond of her yawing under him, the old *Henry*. Through her he could feel the sea. But that wasn't the half of it. Whoever set out to sea had to master the air as well as the water. This was the first thing he had learned, still a young fella, on the family's fishing boats. And always out so early. If you weren't a morning person, you wouldn't hack it. Him, he didn't need much sleep; he looked forward to the night. The night was the time the sky vanished and the cosmos appeared. There wouldn't be much time for stargazing on this night though. Originally, he had set the chances of Charles the Fish arriving safely on the other side at 50:50. But now they were already behind schedule. 65:35. This fish would take some looking after. Golden glittering ghosts drifted lazily by, generously leant their reflection to the water, merged with it. His watch showed he had nearly completed the mandatory half hour of rest that Matilda had to log. He wasn't really involved in the crossing yet. Nor would he be until nightfall. Ah, finally! The world's wind was mounting edgy, chalk-bleached fists, gnarled snowman's toes and noses, bushy brows and earlobes, all slogging it out against each other high in the sky to create the afternoon. Everything must – no, may – rise up. Now!

Charles felt the warmth. He wanted to swim more on the surface, with just the barest of coverings of water. 13:10 said the chronometers? He had reached a plateau now, finely balanced. Over eight hours of rhythm, eight hours of front crawl or breast stroke. He needed new sets of double syllables: "Silas" was out of the question, he'd used up "Hazel."

That left "Brendan." The name reminded him of something, but he hadn't been able to think what for weeks.

Had it something to do with wood? With floating wood? With what Charles was paddling in? It was gloopy. Pine boards, nailed together. Caramelised pine-brown, dark spots left by the branches. Boards like swimming lanes: one up, one down, one up, one down, only he didn't have to turn, he swam nice and straight, a white figure, mobile, skilful, a white, long oval noodle with a cap in this gloopy-wood water, stretching out first one arm, then the other and his legs, quite an elegant figure actually, the way it steered past the almost black knot holes that were to be avoided at all costs, it wouldn't be a good idea to touch that sort of thing, he could do without it, and here he was, swimming in this brown, pine-woody, resinous stuff, but he was making progress, he was slipping along like a worm.

Since the breakfast that he hadn't had at the B&B, time was melting down flanks of waves, flanks of brain, flanks of memory that had previously been hidden to him. Something in his head was becoming ever more malleable, softer. This had never been mentioned in any report, any brochure, any tall tales at the beach.

It was time to stretch out under the warmth of the sun. Afternoon meant that an extra mesh was woven into the sky. The seascape seemed fuller now. Cumulus clouds moved across the firmament to make vedute and theatrical backdrops, old pictures brought back to life. Bridges, crests, cloud arches were forming in the haze.

Winged figures were crashing down.

Stroke, heartbeat, stroke.

His water bottle had been within easy reach. Something inside him panted, something flew. He lay on his back and sucked. The expanse of water shimmered – lay flat – shimmered brightly.

And he was swimming again. Mute, in silver, mottled and small.

He took another suck. It had to be later. Curves and shoulders burgeoned in the ice sky, marriages of monsters and giants filing past every minute. The waves were shedding grey glass like meltwater, green patches were gathering in the hollows, as if each trough were a meadow pushing itself ever forward until it drowned in foam. Charles avoided a branch decorated with seaweed and a milk carton. The great sphere above him was stuffed full of yellowish clouds. He couldn't feel his toes anymore.

On this feed he took his time, two minutes, three, he wanted to see it: the varnish of ice, that so-called sea of clouds, daubed onto a blue that extended upwards for eight kilometres and marked out the limits of the planet. Next to him: his faithful craft. Around and below him: the almost-ice. Above him: a compilation of colour, shot through with a falling, semi-material called light and marked out by fields of ice that were layered over and melting into one another even as they slowly followed the hazy strokes of light downwards. All sorts of dirt came with it. All sorts of dirt was floating about underneath him too. The whales that occasionally crossed the Channel had a heavy dinner. Plastic, effluent, oil.

In the middle: the most unexpected, sharpest of golden glows.

In the middle: him, still swimming.

The *Henry* and her outrigger, the *Henry* and her person, had crossed the English shipping lane. The sun star was hanging close to its zenith, a milky spot, but with a pallid glow. Where its rays struck, the water took on a malicious white sheen. The Channel was playing in a different key to just minutes earlier. The fibres in Charles' muscles were doubling up. They too were singing to a different tune. One note up high, a buzzing, then down low. Under the cover of its own churn the sea was hiding its strength.

In the summer of 1978 they travelled to Sylt for the second time. That was where Abbie told him.

His. Who else's?

Time to be a couple, have a family, a terraced house, on his salary or hers, meaning: him at home with the child? Definitely not. So she and everyone else dependent on him? It must have been sheer enthusiasm that was keeping his mouth agape.

Abbie laughed. She knew exactly what he was thinking: chemistry, research, doctorate. A low salary, high degree of mobility.

Had she really laughed? She rolled up her shirt, showed her belly. Four months. He couldn't see anything. She said, "I'm eating fruit now."

He had noticed that.

He spent the night at the beach. He was in search of strength. Had his girlfriend been waiting for him to guess? And if he had, would they have discussed whether or not to go ahead? Or had that never been a question for Abbie? It certainly didn't seem to be now. Four months. Under the curve of her belly, swimming in its own water, was something that already looked like a tiny person – he could see it in his mind's eye. Her and his child. The sky hung low, the horizon was askew and lengthening its imbalance by the minute. He tensed himself into a ball. Charles wouldn't have known what he wanted even if Abbie had shared the news earlier. He felt left out. That made him angry. Damn it! How well did she know him? And then, just to add to his confusion, there was also the joy: his child. The wind blew, the sand stuck.

Four days passed like this. Then the world slid again.

Can you even call such a sequence of events a sequence of events?

Charles learned more than he had ever wanted to learn. For two years, the summers had returned. Every day had smelled of the future. These weeks of holiday were filled with lightness, and so were they. Maybe they drank even more the second time on Sylt than two summers ago. They also knew a lot more about one another. Life was one big dare. But with each other. That was how he remembered it. It was a memory of his own immortality.

At dawn he had returned to their room feeling irritable. Abbie's eyes betrayed that she had been crying. He decided to give her a few days, although he had no idea what for. That was just what occurred to him. Under the guise of studying for her exams she retreated not just from him but also from Maude and Silas.

When Charles emerged from bed in the mornings, the other two would be at breakfast. Oh, Silas had already jogged to the bakers? No, Maude! They were reading the paper, the *Times* was available, two days old. Abbie, the newfound marmot, was still asleep, three croissants were waiting for her in a paper bag. "She's got a big appetite," said Silas, "why doesn't she get fat, why is it only me?" And in the afternoon, when Charles accompanied him to the post office and they were treating themselves to a fish roll on the harbour wall, he poked him in the ribs: "Strife?" Charles nodded, he didn't want to say anything, nothing at all, so he said, "We've still got your dressing gown."

"She can keep it for now, if she wants."

The following morning, Abbie headed off south with a jam-packed sports bag. The dunes ran in tight waves down that side, there was a new restaurant and a couple of ferry crossings to the other islands. She needed some time alone. To study for some test or other, she said, see you tonight.

They were going to have a barbeque? She would bring along the vegetables, everything that didn't need a fridge.

The bag was really bursting.

"What are you going to do there all day?" he asked. Now he was worried after all. The child in her belly. He thought, "the two of them."

"Study?" said Silas. He didn't believe that for a moment.

"If you ring them, send my greetings," said Maude.

Charles assumed this was a reference to their parents. That Abbie was looking for a phone booth where she could make an international call, to Newcastle.

He didn't give the call any further thought.

"I'm going to lie down with the frogs," said Abbie, "and go 'riddup'. That's about all you lot can understand."

"Phew," said Silas, mock-fanning himself with his hand after she had left, "you could cut that with a knife!"

Afterwards, Charles figured Abbie had wanted to leave the island but, over the course of the day and for whatever reason, had changed her mind. She had been heading back towards them. Her bag contained almost all her clothes, her cheque book, 21 German marks, 46.50 in sterling and her passport.

And 57 French francs.

After they had talked and she had shown him her belly, he had felt like someone who had taken a fall, although he couldn't say where or why. He too needed time, perhaps more than Abbie. Perplexed, he had sat on the ground. In broad daylight. How could the world seem so different? It was asking different things of him. Then, when he wanted to stand back up, more at a loss than downcast, the earth again gave way beneath him and he found himself falling once more. It grew dark. And the falling wouldn't stop. Months later, Charles still felt that the ground had deserted him.

They sat around in Westerland police station.

They had been expecting Abbie back by evening. The clock on the wall was pointing to just before seven o'clock, the window glistening with sunlight.

An accident. They were given Abbie's bag. Large floral pattern. And a plastic bag with corn on the cob, red pepper, crisps.

Maybe she had been blinded. Had felt about for her sunglasses. And saw the bus too late.

That very same evening he got a sore throat. Spent weeks sniffling and coughing. What had happened affected each of them in its own way.

He fled to Oxford. Thanks to his doctoral studies, he could access the lab outside of term time too. His hands worked mechanically, feeling their way round in circles. Vial, pipette, another round of measurements and figures. Every equals sign looked like a road, shooting a jolt through him. Red cars frightened him. He would regularly spend the night in the institute. Chemical processes didn't sleep. He feared every kind of silence, every way of being alone. And yet he couldn't bear anyone trying to talk to him either.

Maude asked him for photos of Abbie. He got a second set made of the prints he had and sent them to her. Her thank-you letter came from Vienna. Eight hours a day, she wrote, she sat at her piano. She wanted to paste together an album for her sister. Once a month she visited her parents. Silas was working in a bank in London, part of his training, he couldn't get away. Charles spoke to him on the phone. Silas wasn't so bad. He was worried about Maude.

Slowly, once term started up again in October, Charles also found his way back into the social life of the college. In the stories doing the rounds he started to see different weights rising and falling. This was new. In the world before Abbie's death there hadn't been any weights. Not like this.

He was numb.

And free. Much too free.

Every night he dreamed of the sisters. Since Sylt he was afraid of losing Maude too. He never used to think like that. Now he couldn't help it. She would probably end up marrying Silas out of grief for Abbie. And yet the two of them really got on best when they were only playing. Wasn't that exactly what he had heard in their music? He wrote Maude that letter, Oxford, 12 November 1978. Wrote about Abbie and Silas in order to show her who Silas was. Abbie had never explicitly claimed to have slept with her sister's boyfriend. Charles was lying. And yet it didn't seem to be a total untruth. Silas, notoriously a ladies' man. My goodness, that at least must be evident to Maude. Yes, he was sowing discord. He wanted to wake her up. Show how different he was. And so he stood in front of the slit in the post-box, so red, so angular and narrow, and let the envelope go.

South of Rantum, Abbie had avoided a bus and skidded off the road. Her car, a rental Ford Fiesta, had overturned. Abbie, with no seatbelt; Abbie, with alcohol in her bloodstream.

"Did you ever notice that she drank?" the younger of the police officers asked. With effort, in English.

They shrugged their shoulders.

"Never met any English tourists, by the sound of things," said his older colleague, in German. He didn't suspect that any of the English party could understand him. The younger officer turned red.

After a while, this officer started turning up in Charles' dreams. He didn't understand where the man came from, nor what he should mean. He was pale, looked neither sad nor curious. If only the policeman had said a single word, it might have provided some kind of explanation. The German was roughly the same age as the four of them (Charles still thought like that, both awake and asleep, "the four of them") and didn't move his lips.

After the accident they had remained on the island. They were required to do so, in case there were any questions. Charles was offered a smaller room in the house, without a balcony. It was important to be near one another, even if they were only reading or going for a walk; without ever having agreed it, they all stayed within earshot. Maude rang her parents often, all of a sudden there was so much to organize, and keeping busy like this seemed to provide some relief. And then hours of emptiness prevailed once more. Someone did the shopping, even though they ate almost nothing. From 4 p.m. they started drinking, any earlier was forbidden. Did Maude cry? Charles didn't see it and didn't ask Silas; he was totally dry himself, both on the inside and the outside, and spent most of the time asleep. At least the world in his sleep was unchanged for those first few days -- until the younger policeman turned up in his dreams and, with this, the knowledge that something was irretrievably lost. Slowly this crept into Charles' waking consciousness and extinguished the pictures of "the four of us," one by one.

He calls it eyes of light: exposed to the sun's reflection on the water for so many years that it shows up on your iris.

Brendan, so near. Yes indeed, he can see him perfectly now. His goggles had been fogged up. Not any longer, right, it's all alright on the night, eh-eh, best mate.

Brendan says he called him several times.

"Are you ok, Charles?"

No he can't have another feed.

The pilot points to the right.

A wooden boat is drifting ten feet away from Charles. Jerkily, a middle-aged man is tugging at the oars. There's a girl sitting in the bow, about ten years old, with long blond plaits.

Cedric announces the coastguard is on its way. They were looking after Charles.

He just has to steer clear.

"And go!"

When he briefly and – so Cedric can't see it – only half turns around, he finds himself looking into the large, matt-black eye of a camera. The girl, desperately craning her neck, is pointing the lens at him.

He goes underwater. No one can cruise about like that in the Channel, and certainly not in a rowing boat. And with a child to boot!

For a few more strokes he hears the boat as it moves away; and then that almost mellow sound that reminds him of freshwater vanishes. The way the oars stir eddies in the liquid mass, the gentle lapping of the waves, the warmth radiating from the sun. Or is it bursting out of his body? He has given himself over so totally to gasping for air that he has lost all hearing, tastes only iron and blood.

"How do you feel?"

"Eh?"

He was supposed to take an ibuprofen. But he wanted paracetamol, that British wonder-drug straight from the supermarket. For sore muscles, flesh, soul. Brendan was asking if he was too hot.

"I am a teaspoon," he replied.

"You are incoherent," said Cedric.

Fantastic, finally to lob this word at someone else. *Incoherent!* As a child Cedric had heard it so often that he knew exactly what it meant. The old fella down there was properly losing it. "I am a teaspoon!" Maybe his, Cedric's, wilful hands did generally do something different to his feet, but he was more in control of his tongue, that was for sure! Blokes like Charles literally needed a whole sea to work through their issues. He would rather stroke Helen's pug. And Helen. He threw a few stones into the salty tide: plop, plop, plop. Exactly why he'd brought them. They sank nicely. You – that is to say, he – just knew this world was wonky. For example, the way this teacher-woman had torn off her clothes just now. A hen like her, and specifically of her age, shouldn't be asking for it anymore. But there she stood, half naked, in front of him and sunburned like nobody's business! She was peeling from top to bottom. Was he in his prime? Did he have to see that? He had muttered "no animal cruelty," she had looked at him as if she were amazed he could even talk. Otherwise she had just felt about for her sunglasses and pretended not to have heard him.

"How's ibuprofen for home comforts?," Charles shouted up the ship's flank.

Surprised, he looked up after his voice. Sounded pretty strong. Matilda noted something down. Apropos hot: she was only wearing a bikini top and shorts now. Then it struck him that a hot sensation in your hands and legs was one of the symptoms of hypothermia.

He mustn't let himself get too hot under any circumstances.

"Home comforts." Was it that hard to understand?

Finally, someone laughed. Cedric? Writing appeared on the whiteboard: Paracetamol = for fever = lowers body temperature. We're not *crazy*!

He took the ibuprofen that was swung down to him in a piece of string knotted on to the end of the rod. It looked like bait.

On the board, a new message penned itself: Arrival time = 1.30 a.m. He was slower than he thought. Now, on the open stretch. They didn't tell him, he figured that out himself.

Was anything else happening? Pine wood, resinous-tough. He thought about those chameleon legs like macaroni in Oxford's Natural History Museum. Was that what he already looked like? Was his skin blue? Or transparent? For a few moments he couldn't see himself until he realised that his goggles had fogged up again. He closed his eyes and imagined lying on the lawn in front of the museum next to the glistening plaster casts of dinosaur footprints. On days like today, you spent your time in that venerable university city sitting on folding chairs around one of those practical, weighted picnic blankets that don't blow away, drinking Pimm's and eating soggy-sweet strawberries and cream.

His water bottle was swinging towards him. Another pill.

When he swallowed, darts of pain shot from his raw lips into his mucous membranes. Inch by inch the salt was eating its way down his throat.

"Not your fault, mate," Cedric signalled from the boat, meaning the 1.30 a.m. arrival time.

Charles swallowed.

"Drifted … further … than … expected."

The bottle had spewed out peach. Gradually the flavour came through. The dratted tablet was stuck half way down Charles' throat, the piece of sky to the left corner of the wheelhouse was turning poison yellow, as if it too had swallowed rotten peach mush. He looked to the right, turned through 180 degrees. The light was dividing itself up into batches, falling from the sky. Some of the batches strained towards each other; in other places all brightness was being slurped out of the atmosphere by invisible robotic suction.

Two in the afternoon. A little dark for that.

Far too bloody dark for that. The horizon heavy, a strong green-grey wall.

It couldn't be much longer until they reached Z. The middle of the Channel. The zone that was given over to rubbish.

The wall was growing, bulging inwards. Ship, man, and what else there was, they were all drifting under the glass bell that sat on the sea. On its inner skin jagged shapes jostled alongside one another, lit up, disappeared, only to flash back just seconds later as if constellated in reverse, slightly to the side of their original place. A swarm of electricity, distant lightning strikes, momentary illumination.

"Bit early, love, for a Hallowe'en mask," Cedric cast in a stage whisper to Matilda. Frothy seas, every which way. The teacher's face had turned a beautiful algal shade.

"I leave the mask on all year. It's so wonderfully free of wrinkles," she said.

Cedric laughed. Well look at that, the old bird had a sense of humour! He gave her a thumbs up. A practical gesture to spare words, but also multi-functional: the sign was used on choppy seas to wish one another happy vomiting.

Grey-green fences rolled across the sky, the Channel flickered with silver weals. Wave after wave collapsed, the whole water plateau was sinking. The calm before the storm. He didn't know what caused this, but now he certainly knew what it was. Black baroque clouds, the drama queens of a storm, obviously only hung over land. On the sea the storm was less constrained, faster, wild. It pounded forth, no transition.

Brendan appeared on deck in a yellow oilskin, his face hidden under a cap that was held in place by a bootlace wrapped around his forehead. The other two had disappeared. The wind snatched every word out of the skipper's mouth.

Charles knew it too: the first lightning strike and he would be out. Over!

His pilot was gesticulating, shouting. That wasn't what he meant? There was something else?

The end of the swim … delay … getting delayed … more … bigger …

 To fi … against the tides …

… loops, i… higher the … fa…

"Hours," Charles heard

"… parallel!"

Brendan was drawing on the whiteboard, the rain was beating against it. Indelible ink. Charles really could have done without this. Then the wind snatched the board out of the oil figure's hand. Which didn't matter a jot, because he had hung it around his neck.

… parallel

… he, Charles,

… to his …

endpoint

–

–

The shiny surface displayed: arrival = 2 – 4 a.m.

That late now? It must be the storm driving them back towards England. At the time of the morning that was written on the board the receding tide would be so strong that someone of Charles' age, already over twenty hours in the water, would never make it. They had discussed this scenario before they left, he remembered.

And?

"And!" (= croaked) (= him)

Whether he still wanted to continue, now?

The piece of the Channel ahead of Charles was twitching irregularly, in-between lay pigeon-grey, deadened strips of inexplicably calm water, scattered with shiny globules of paste. The clouds had already begun to lift slightly, Charles saw something akin to expanse. Was the man responsible for his life asking him now, in the middle of this bad weather, in order to test his strength? Was he trying to save himself the bother of having to insist on finishing early, giving up? It was clear there was no way to negotiate in these conditions. Here and there, lightning streaked through the thick grey of the storm front; as if in a film, the full-scale discharges lit up the southeast, where the firmament had shrunk to a thin line. Many of the forks of light banded together, playing at being human, over-extended, deadly, yellow.

He gave his pilot the thumbs-up. Arrival between two and four in the morning. That would be between twenty-one and twenty-three hours swimming in total. That had been done before.

Brendan pointed to the sky, nodded. The storm was moving off, it was only raining now. Rain is better when you're in the water than on deck. Charles had studied films of Channel crossings, lots of them, all recorded from the accompanying boat, and so he knew that in all probability they could no longer see him now, even if they were pretending to be in control of the situation. Only the ridiculous light sticks would give them any point of reference. The wetness from above didn't bother Charles in the slightest, quite the opposite, he had the impression the rain was calming the tidal swell. Ahead of itself, night, half-cooked; he was straining for night-time proper. Then he would finally be on his own, just him and the water. No eyes, no constant feedback. Then he would no longer be battling on a stage.

But in real life instead?

Ridiculous. As if this weren't real enough.

Or would the stage simply flip over, point down to the bottom?

He relaxed. Began to give into the depths a touch now. Fight off all fear. Fear constricted every vessel. From now on he would come up for air as infrequently as possible. Save energy, into the bargain.

Under water, the rain was transformed. Gave a tap, a light kiss, and dissipated. So gentle. For the second time, this crossing was beautiful. Cheered, Charles imagined drifting in one vast mind. His body was melting into everything around him. Noiselessly, big ships ploughed their way behind the curtain of droplets in the world above. He had become more porous, perhaps also a bit holey; he could sense the ships without seeing them.

After reading his letter in November 1978, Maude took more time for her next visit to England. She travelled from Newcastle to London, to Silas. Charles assumed she was having it out with her boyfriend. Abbie pregnant. His child? And other women in his life? Admittedly, he was only imagining all this. She had never said a word about it, neither then nor later. But after her visit to London she had dropped in on Charles in Oxford. Because they had all changed. Because she needed him, at last. That was the cleaned-up version. He remembered how they had been erecting a Christmas tree with considerable effort on Broad Street when he just wanted to nip through and go round the back of Balliol to pick Maude up from the bus station on time.

They spent two days together, nothing happened. Charles had moved into a new room, the rooms in college were swapped every autumn. It was quite like his old accommodation; the corner room comprised two large picture windows and overlooked the long college quadrangle with the holm-oak. Maude slept in Charles' bed, he took the mattress on the floor. Maude kept her t-shirt on, her tights. He wore pyjamas. They were no longer as raw with shock as in August. They took comfort now in holding on to one another.

Abbie's name wasn't mentioned once. Nor did they speak about Silas. Their past in any case had become far too large for them. They needed new places. Maude practiced on the organ in the college chapel. That was somewhere Charles had never gone with Abbie. They also went to the Natural History Museum. The sea already connected them. In the museum's naves of glass and iron it returned, but in a tolerable, indirect way. The muteness of the creatures that had crawled out of the salt water matched their own. Bound together in their silence, they walked around the exhibits. Sometimes his proximity to Maude flashed in Charles like an electric pulse, for fragments of a second everything was simultaneously and fundamentally present, the chick in the large, speckled egg in the glass case, the fossilized fern frond that had unfurled in all its green glory with the light of ten thousand years ago, the white noise of the trees in University Park behind the building, the hum of the visitors beside them.

One morning, a cart with a narrow, unexpectedly long telescopic ladder was parked in the left nave. The man on the end of it was tying bones onto a barely visible string. Whale skeletons were being hung up, the final two were still lying on the floor, flat as a pancake, all the little bones carefully pieced together. Only when lifted under the ceiling did they become round, float.

"The first music was played on grasses and bones," said Maude.

"The first human music," said Charles.

Whales sang in a different way.

In the night-time they lay in each other's arms. Nothing happened. Everything happened. Maude had come to visit him. Him.

Gradually he noticed the white noise. It wasn't going away. It was increasing. A nasty grating sound had started up now too. He took a deep breath, dived under, three feet at most. And yet everything went dark. Differently dark to what he had ever seen. Think, Charles. Something's rolling around above you, too slow-moving to be a boat. And that ringing, that scraping? A shark? Nonsense. There weren't any in the Channel, this devil's strait was too cold for the sensible creatures. Couldn't be a hovercraft either, too small. In any case, that sort of error, his swim route crossing the path of a regular boat, that would never have happened to the experienced Brendan.

Astonished, he realised he ought to be afraid, but he wasn't. Darkness was turning circles above him. It was rustling, hustling, almost smacking its lips. He began to conserve his breath.

It wasn't getting any brighter.

He seemed caught in the same grind as that thing. He trained his senses on himself once more.

Still no signs of panic. Only his head was expanding from lack of air.

He saw nothing. So he closed his eyes. He knew which way was up. Didn't he know that anyway? How many minutes can you hold your breath? Depends on the circumstances, said the eager pupil in his head.

He found it funny. Not the situation, the eager voice.

His chest grew warm. The warmth was branching out to both sides, flowing into his arms. It didn't feel right, but pleasant. He stretched his arms. He flowed after his arms, something was pulling him. A shirt was floating above him. His head was enormous. His head flowed into the shirt. Floated up the left sleeve. Lucky for you that the shirt isn't shrinking, said the voice. It was still there, albeit remarkably tame due to the lack of air. His head followed his hand. His body was weightless. This too he found logical.

He? Hand, arm, head slipped up the sleeve.

Blue was streaming towards him. Brendan's eyes up close, almost at the same level as him.

"What the fucking hell!"

Something was gasping.

Him, Charles. So he was still here.

"Oh yes: fuck!"

The pilot had lowered the lifeboat and rowed over to Charles. Just in time, Charles checked the instinct to grab on to the side of the dinghy.

"Charles!"

"Ye … yeah."

Charles, still spluttering. His skipper had dropped down in the lifeboat to find him more easily.

"Flotsam?" said Brendan. Well, Charles was some quick thinker. A corrugated iron roof!

Rusty, sharp. Cut through your throat if you were stupid enough to get in its way. Came at crazy double speed, out of nowhere, just careered over, damned rain, wind, rubbish, so they hadn't been able to warn him.

Diving! The best – only – thing he could have done.

Brendan said he was proud of him. The rain had worn itself out. It had only been a squall. A squall a way off. They had got through it.

"You'll make it, fella, right to the end!"

"Sure?"

"Sure."

The waves, softer now than before the bad weather, were licking all around him. Dogs' tongues? Miniature sleeves from a blue shirt. This he could make out clearly. Didn't have to say it though. The *Henry* had taken on quite a pitch. Overall, a calming scene.

An honourable fish.

Well on his way: Charles the Fish. He laughed. Brendan the Ancient Mariner had no idea where he had been. He, Charles, had an easy laugh. The dangerous part of the crossing had begun. Yes, his pilot probably thought so too. All Brendan had to do was take a look at his watch.

A bit crowded here, Charles said between breaths. He was breathing normally again now, not gasping.

His partner-for-life was rowing along beside him. The *Henry* accompanied them. No more time to lose. Charles, how he was swimming again. A pity that his ferrying fellow didn't get the crowded joke.

They zoomed in, zoned out, zig-zagged their way through Z. A state's national sovereignty above ground extended between 40 and 70 miles up into space and the same amount down into the bedrock of the planet. Europe was mapped, scanned, measured, divided.

Except for Z.

Z was nothing, either above or below. Z, the ultimate, ultimatum. Z, an N turned on its side: no-man's-land. Nothing. Or maybe also W? God's most perfect wasteland. Once a week, specially equipped ships pushed the rubbish out of the French and English territorial zones and into the nothing that bordered each sovereignty equally.

Z, after eleven hours of swimming. Charles had been looking forward to it. Halfway. If not exactly in terms of time. Plastic, metal, junk.

Charles asked Brendan as he rowed along easily beside him, whether he would live with a woman who had had first one man and then another and now wanted the first one back again. Not as a simple swap, mind, but rather a double bill, as it were: have one back and keep the other. And this as a lasting, wonderfully simultaneous solution. One woman, two men, all living together in the same house.

Brendan pulled the oars through the water. Slows the thoughts, Charles figured. When he had one ear free (= above water) for the third time, he discerned a "maybe." When the ear came back up for the sixth time, his pilot said, it depended on the woman.

The pilot: some are just like that.

The pilot: that they were worth it.

A late revelation this time, thought Brendan. Not bad down here, the water looking like it had just been washed through with blue and you so close to it that your hand was wet with even the slightest flick. At some point, every candidate starts telling you what was in it for them. They might still try to hide their reasons even when they were in the water, but eventually they had to talk. This one here, Charles, he was dogged, obstinate too. The kind that got that extra bit of strength at the end, if they found their strength at all. What that depended on was beyond him. No one person could look that far into somebody else. Not even here. Here, you really weren't looking anywhere in particular. He was happy with that. He could look past Cedric. No need to get annoyed. There he had been again, standing at the railing, throwing stones into the Channel. Overwrought, the boy, still. As a child he would have spent the first three hours chasing around the deck. Actually a great kid too. Some dirty angel had kissed him! Practical, the way Cedric never slept. And then once, in the night, that sentence had come out of nowhere. His cousin had said it to him or maybe it was his own idea: inside, everyone is thick, soft, darkness.

Emphasis on "soft."

"The sea is singing," Brendan told his swimmer, "listen."

"What?" Charles shouted back.

He stretched. It seemed as if the rain had stretched the water too. The *Henry*'s engine was ticking over, an uneventful (please) afternoon lay ahead of them. Please, please me! He didn't even feel sick anymore. Brendan was rowing with just one hand, trying with his other to ferret the weather forecast out of his trouser pocket. The paper flapped in the wind, it was impractical, but nevertheless important. Brendan had explained to Charles that they would have to consult this morning's data. Any idiot could find the latest information online. The skipper was comparing the old forecast with the current state of play in order to judge the quality of the forecast for the evening.

"Looks ideal. Even for Matilda's sensitive stomach."

The log-lady, strikingly pale, had just re-appeared at the railing.

Charles thought it was about time that less started happening again. Half full, half empty? He was swimming, swimming strongly. Not seeing, not feeling. He wanted to be further on, he wanted it to be dark. Long before he realised what was happening, he felt the water vibrating.

Only when his rhythm allowed it did he come up for air and open his eyes. The lifeboat was bobbing empty next to the *Henry*. Brendan was suspended half way down the ship's short ladder, as if glued in place.

And shouting. The word began with "f."

Otherwise all was noticeably quiet. Charles picked up on that too.

The waves swelled, the wind whistled. The engine of the *Henry* stood still.

Stroke, stroke, the next chance to look: their esteemed pilot was beside himself with rage.

"Stop, Charles, Stop!"

Brendan: "Fuck!"

Brendan: He should have known. One load of rubbish usually heralded another.

The *Henry* was drifting, at the whim of the waves.

The lifeboat, held by a rope, bobbed to its own rhythm.

Charles the Fish trod water. He wasn't allowed to continue without the ship. Cedric and Brendan were discussing the situation on deck, he could see their arms, shoulders, their heads put together.

He swam closer to the ship, trod water vertically. The discussion didn't take long. His pilot took off his trousers, pulled his shirt over his head.

Fabulous silence. Even the wind was barely whispering. All the better for Charles down in the water, now he could hear every word spoken on deck. Quite the men of action, those men busily beckoned Matilda over to them. Could she steer? Start the engine, when Brendan gave her a sign? Charles swore. Cedric climbed down into the lifeboat, helpfully still rocking up and down in the waves, and announced with a surfeit of cheer that this catastrophic turn of events would be fixed in no time.

Even by English standards, the lie was crass. The ship's captain, down to his underwear, let himself fall with a sigh into the sea from the middle rung of the ladder. On his way, he wetted Cedric. Charles was happy to share the cold with them both.

Welcome, fish.

Brendan had to free the screw underwater by hand; the know-it-all teacher in the wheelhouse, so Cedric said, was licensed to drive a car. It was her job to establish whether the engine would start again. The two of them had to stick exactly to the agreed schedule, testing every five minutes, otherwise Matilda would rip off Brendan's hand at the touch of a button.

She could warrant this wannabe punk was whispering something about her appearance to Charles, she could practically hear it; after thirty-two years in a school you hear everything. Mr Aquarius, by contrast, suited her down to the ground: reliably mute. Of course she could turn on an engine. She could whistle with her fingers, repair an organ, and her first-aid skills were legendary. Would Cedric like a demonstration of her mouth-to-mouth resuscitation? She would offer him that when he was back on board. A rib-breaking routine!

Cedric meanwhile was rowing snappily towards France: "A routine operation, Charles, ten minutes at most, and we'll have our screw loose again. Ha ha."

Charles pursed, routine, his lips together.

Just how many times did you have to hit rock bottom and plough on?

How much of this could you take over the course of one day? Was there a limit?

He was in favour of a limit.

For weeks after Abbie's accident he had felt that he needed to crawl onto land, back to life. He missed her more than he might have thought. Her death had collapsed a wall that none of them had even suspected existed, triggering something that broke over them more fully and more hotly than even the rush of bodily heat brought about by a major shock. It had made that thing called youth evaporate on the spot.

He wanted to salvage at least one thing for himself: the right woman. The port that the senior butler sold at a discount in his college was dark and sweet, headache guaranteed. Not knowing what Maude was doing drove him wild. Neither of them had a telephone in their room. He had to use one of the phone booths at the Martyrs' Memorial, the only ones in the city for international calls. The queue wound several times around the memorial. When it was finally his turn, after an hour or more's wait, his fingers were sometimes so cold that he could hardly dial the number. The booths stank, the machine gobbled up the coins, the people waiting outside stared in.

The post-box had been remarkably discreet in swallowing up the letter to Maude. Whenever he passed by, he would stare at it. There stood his future on the ground before him: terrifyingly, blindingly red.

Was he lying in the letter? On one of the afternoons on Sylt, Abbie, Silas and Maude had walked down to the village without him, he hadn't wanted to join. That was their routine, they went shopping in varying constellations, depending on what was needed. He remembered sitting reading on the balcony when Silas and Abigail returned in a temper without Maude: she had turned off for the beach, leaving them to lug everything themselves! The two of them carried the bags into Silas' and Maude's room, the only one with a fridge, and because the two balconies were right next to each other and all the doors open, Charles heard them joking and deciding what to drink up first. Then everything went quiet, dreadfully quiet, until about a quarter of an hour later Silas stepped out onto the balcony, freshly showered and with a towel around his waist. Abbie followed shortly afterwards, wearing his bath-robe and carrying a shiny new yellow thermos. They grinned at Charles, he was sure they were trying to play a trick on him, so he played one right back by slapping his forehead and shouting out he'd nearly forgotten, he was supposed to be meeting Maude. And off he rushed.

He actually did find Maude almost straight away on the beach. Past the village (coincidentally? intuitively!) Charles had taken the right turn, not out to the mudflats but towards the side facing the open sea. As he walked south along the North Sea he was no longer so sure about the nature of the joke that the two of them had been playing. Abbie seemed different to him, first coquettish (not something he associated with her), and then disproportionately quiet. Maude was ly-ing on her towel asleep; he sat down beside her on the sand and looked at her for a while, at some point she also looked at him. Neither said a word, they didn't touch, he was just happy being close to her. He assumed Maude had also heard about the pregnancy.

Only Silas was carrying on with the old, light-hearted life.

Charles told Maude about the yellow thermos flask. She knew about it, of course, she had done the shopping with them. The fact that his girlfriend every now and then had mumbled in her sleep for months, a short word that he couldn't make out, something like 'les' or 'tes' or 'text' – he kept that to himself. That evening he tried once more to speak to Abbie. Calmer this time. She hesitated, listened, but didn't say anything, and realizing that he didn't really know what to make of a future that kept on separating out into a 'him', 'her', and 'it', he happily agreed to her suggestion of waiting until they were back home.

Two days later, Abbie lay in Westerland hospital and no-one could help her any more. Her death didn't bring anything crashing down on Charles, Maude or Silas (even if Charles would have liked to think so and was plagued by a lurching sensation). The world carried on as if nothing had happened. They returned from the police station to a reality where the fridge in Maude's and Silas' room hummed loudly at night and yellow thermos flasks were on special offer in the supermarket.

Above water he opened his eyes roughly once a minute, on every fifth breath. He was taking breaths more frequently now. The sequence of images generated by opening and closing his eyelids formed a jerky motion picture. The *Henry*, finally moving once more, was chugging more quietly than ever. Brendan, operating underwater, had succeeded in cutting free half a lobster net that had locked teeth with the screw. With a knife clamped between his jaws he had repeatedly dived down to the rotor. Matilda and Cedric, unexpectedly united by a common interest, had drawn the scene in a comic strip on the whiteboard for Charles. The captain a pirate!

They were a wonderful team. Cedric sketched the figures, edgy fellas, and Matilda looked after the cartoon framing, ship and text.

The film that Charles' eyes were creating consisted of long sequences of darkness. The breath-pictures of just a few seconds were over-exposed. Closing his eyes resulted in a stronger focus internally, even his hearing turned inwards, into his body, while his arms and legs kept on striking out-wards, trying to grasp what lay beyond. It gave Charles a heightened sense of both him and not-him. The film that his eyes were generating also showed him two things: his dark self and, in the momentary, flickering shots, the others. Those others were the keepers of reality, the one that counted as real and circumscribed the boat, its people, and the Charles the three crew members were observing. He could imagine what they saw: a slender figure in the water with a black hat and recurrent appetite, a tiddler that would take the bait every half hour. Clouds like candyfloss drifted lazily across the firmament. On the Channel's blue-grey skin, branched pat-terns were jigging back and forth, looking to become part of the picture-capture. They were what you might call nature, unavoidable reflection. This was the moment when the social world intervened in Charles' Channel crossing with a new message. The whiteboard snapped back down over the rail-ing.

The message consisted of two words that he couldn't un-derstand. He could understand each on its own but not what they meant together. Two words, two syllables, each begin-ning with an "s."

He had learned by heart: after Z, a sequence of buried sandbanks forced a more changeable rhythm on the narrow passage of water. Not something he had given any further consideration.

The waves were taking on a deep blue hue again, and on their sides hollows were forming that resembled the hips of an undernourished animal. It looked like the sea was taking on dents. Ever more waves were collapsing into their own troughs and flattening out. They were being extinguished as if they had never existed in the first place and it wasn't long until the last little ripple had died away.

The water relaxed. Charles could sense it relenting. Everything became smooth. Like a glaze masterfully applied with a silicon spatula. Now he was shooting forward on every stroke.

The wind had died.

Still sea, said the board.

Then it was as if all the air were vanishing.

Only he, Charles, was still breathing.

The Channel lay motionless, like cold soup in a pan. The Knife Pirate himself was noiselessly lowering the freshly wiped, silver-framed board towards Charles until the letters were mirrored in the ever more intensely blue water: Still sea!

Hadn't he read about this sea-watery still-stand in a novel? Or was it on one of the Channel websites? Unusual, unexplained.

Then he remembered: Brendan. Brendan the Navigator, the Irish monk who had set off to seek paradise, told of it. Hazel had written an essay in school about the pious adventurer's journey of discovery, Charles had helped her. Back and forth across the oceans the obsessive explorer had led his monks, seven years long, determined, powerful, legendary. Hazel had found the figure from the early sixth century spectacular in every way: he had discovered Greenland and probably landed in Canada, describing the most mythical islands of the globe and, above all, of the imagination. Charles hadn't been able to make much of it, a world without evidence was foreign to him. Now, he was astonished to realize that something which up until yesterday he would have cast aside without a second thought had a rather comforting allure. There was this person who had discovered a crystal pillar at the bottom of the ocean, marvelled at a city built out of scales, tranquillity, and sparkle, and experienced a still sea, the silence of the water. This silence was the sea's most philosophical minute – the one where it contradicted itself.

Pure fantasy. But wasn't the stillness expanding ahead of them? Weren't his three crossing companions witnessing it too?

Certainly only he, Charles, was swimming in it.

It was as if the world were growing.

As if it were becoming over-whole.

Brendan had killed the *Henry*'s engine and grabbed a pair of binoculars. A mute seaman still wanted to be a useful seaman. Waterman Charles' advantage: he didn't have to see the stillness, he sensed it all over.

Transformed into its own stillness, the sea resembled a clearing in a forest. Almost entirely transparent, a few clouds cast wispy-grey, long-distance runners into the afternoon sky. Charles' legs were doing almost no work, his arms were resting.

One minute of wonder. There had to be time for that.

It was as still now as if snow were falling on salt water. He had experienced this once during his winter training; a total coming-to-rest that kept regenerating itself out of every flake, every veil of dispersed snow. He never would have imagined that something like this could be possible in the sea, that element that was constantly touching itself because it needed to establish its own balance from within. Everything seemed poised, peaceable. Whizzy wizardry, said Charles' syllable-counting voice. The afternoon sun was beating down, nothing was less likely than snow, and yet the stillness reached across the seasons.

From his aching thighs came a sensation of eternal present, with sun and shade intertwining. The water was showing the most exact pictures imaginable of the clouds, interrupted and distorted only by the staggered, angular shadow cast by the *Henry*. The people on deck were conferring. In the stillness, every word hung individually in the air.

"Charles?"

"Charles, listen. You're okaaaayyy?"

He laughed. The laugh slid a few centimetres above the surface of the water, died away.

Let's kick off.

Wind? Hidden in the shadows of the cliffs, which in turn were nothing more than shadows of nothing? Charles shook his head.

But his pilot was right (as regrettable as reassuring): something was wedging its way between the glittering mirrors of atmosphere and water. It was a whistle, infinitely thin, spreading out like the flattest sheet of filo pastry between the watery expanse and the air suspended above it. An invisible hand had passed over the tide to becalm and bewitch it, now this hand was melting away. It grew thinner and thinner, and the Channel remembered itself.

Charley, listen!

He did.

Sea sounded like seer.

It was, so much was now perfectly clear, a mistake, to seek an all-seeing soul in the sea.

It lived on top of it. One membrane, spread over the oceans as they embraced the globe.

Thin and drawn out ever more thinly, without any sound.

"You're okaaaayyy?"

He laughed. Charley! Charley-Darley. Darling Charles.

His laugh slid thinly on and on over the sea's skin. The sky was floating just inches above it. He was swimming.

H_2O, rule 6: Throw one hand in front of the other until you bite into sand.

Brendan shouted: "You're only kicking!"

"He's moving alright," said the woman's voice.

The cold was creeping through Charles' fat like cracks branching across ice. It was biting through.

"Yes," he shouted up the smooth, white wall.

Cramp in his left foot, Charles stretched it out. A wooden pallet, caramel brown and rubbed to a sheen, bobbed past him. Nice of it. He almost waved. The human body consisted of seventy percent water. In the other thirty percent resided an animal that craved only one thing: to survive.

He nestled his face into the shadow of a wave, he kicked, he drank.

No question, shade and wind had returned. Charles signalled to the deck: "Take a second ... cup!"

Captain Webb had not been able to walk for a week after his crossing. The ring of naked, raw flesh around his neck had tormented him for even longer, sea ulcers, as they were known. Fish were familiar with the problem, Charles was sure of it. The first sign of weakness and something starts chewing on you. There had been excellent reasons for crawling onto land.

"… from feed to feed, until something pretty scratches your balls!"

"Oh," he murmured, "Freda, I hear you."

Thank you, brain. Brain of Charles. Sentences were floating like inflated diamonds, no, luminous pufferfish, through the Channel's sky towards him.

Rule 11: Think it's warm.

He thought: when I get out, I'll be rattling.

Charley, Man of Iron.

Maude opened the door, even the corridor smelled different to before, that short, shared before in 8 Portland Terrace. The woman standing in the doorway appeared composed. He was overcome by the desire to draw her close, as if that would make everything undone, as if he could tear her away from it all, but he got a grip on himself, and the dog cavorted between his legs, or was it the other way around, Sampo got under his feet and the momentary impulse faded. Instead, Charles reached for Maude's arm. She had called him in, no "asked" for a conversation, and here he was.

She shook off his hand.

But let him in.

Silas was there, she said.

The majority of Charles' things were also still there. Now that he had come, this much was clear to him, something would have to change. He owed himself that.

His wife led the way downstairs to the kitchen. The black and white floor had been Charles' choice; they had found the walnut dresser together in Camden Market, the over-large dining table too. The creeping plants on the slope were running wild, the jasmine needed water, did nobody see this? The windows had been done, double glazing instead of the traditional English sash. She had arranged this without asking him.

Nor did she ask him how he wanted his tea. Dunk the bag for one minute, add a generous slosh of milk.

He took the mug. He would have preferred it if his taste had changed. He, Charles, had changed. His feelings were sloshing around. Men didn't go through the menopause, more's the pity, he would have liked to write his experiences off as that. Sometimes he almost wanted to cry, he would find himself inexplicably sad of an evening, sitting leaning against the terraced wall of his Oxford pad.

He was moody, a state of mind quite new to him. There were mornings when he didn't even want to get out of bed. Crept further under the duvet. Started hallucinating about Chopin and watching films with Benedict Cumberbatch.

In early April he had celebrated his birthday with "friends," mostly colleagues, students, no family. He had laughed, joked, been ironic, a professor with grey stubble. The standard Oxford academic corduroy trousers weren't for him. Richie, a doctoral student out jogging, had spotted him at seven that morning on a park bench in Christ Church Meadow. Oh, he replied, he was taking a walk, watching the crows. His cold-water training, his plan, was a well-kept secret. After two hours, all the guests had noiselessly, efficiently dispersed. Very British, an art form in its own right: social evaporation.

That was how friends worked here.

And how things would continue?

In the empty house, Charles felt hot and cold and rational and like he wanted to cry. Since living alone, he had become aware how little life he had left, he sensed his mortality. But also Maude's. He regularly took himself to task for this: *de facto* nothing had been any different before he moved out, but this sort of rationalised equation offered no relief to his misery; it deepened it.

"I filled Hazel in a bit," said Maude.

About the past?

"About now," said Maude. "That we are meeting on amicable terms."

She didn't ask him what he was up to these days. She surely assumed that he had buried himself in his lab. Charles, predictably boring. Thanks to his swimming plans he could look her in the eye. How wrong she was! His Maude. How familiar she looked. Just as he had known her. She didn't look better. He was relieved. Definitely not better.

Nor worse.

He hoped he didn't look worse for the move. He too had written to Hazel.

Maude shrugged her shoulders. She had rung Hazel. What was he thinking?

Charles, quite daft. Clearly he was nervous. The thought of Silas in the house, somewhere above him, did not have a calming effect.

Was he lying in bed? The bed that had belonged to Charles and Maude? On his, the husband's, side? And what about the reading chair that Charles had bought to celebrate moving in? It was creepy when you started to think about the details. It was so – profane.

His students followed their own lives and the lives of others online. Measured their heart rate while jogging, sleeping, having sex. Their person reflected back to them in their devices. He understood what was precious about that. He used one too. Nevertheless, he was holding out for some other kind of inner life. There had to be more left of it than just making tea in the *practical* – English way.

Hazel had written that she was sorry he had moved out. She hoped her parents could solve the crisis (crisis? Hadn't Maude mentioned Silas then? Or did Hazel assume, like her mother, that the situation could be resolved – with Silas?). He shouldn't worry about her. Could she do anything for him?

He had felt her energy, her life-force. How busy she was. Had been happy to see this – and lonely.

"Am I here to talk about Hazel with you?" he asked Maude.

Who was sitting opposite him in leggings and thick socks, her legs tucked in, both heels on the edge of her chair, safely encapsulated, her mug balanced on her knees. And was looking at him with a mildly amused expression.

Ah, Charles! Did he not understand, or not want to understand?! He was here because she had something to tell him. She would have told him before he had decreed a time-out, had he not run away so quickly.

And he would be doing the same again any moment, he said.

She appeared not to have heard him at all. Now, she said, she had been thinking. She still wanted him to know.

It wasn't long ago. Last year. Hadn't he just been saying there were too many letters in their story?

But before she began: Another cup of tea?

She put out shortbread from a new, red tin. The double-decker bus was stuck to the fridge the right way up, clasping a shopping list.

Did Charles remember the beige-coloured envelope from a London solicitor? It arrived in March last year.

Of course he remembered it. He had plucked it from the carpet behind the front door and carried it into the kitchen, where Maude was having her first and he his second Saturday breakfast. Solicitors. Always a shock at first.

Too many letters, said his not-yet-ex-wife, maybe he was right, she said. She was holding her second cup of tea. She had put the first in the sink. Dirty.

The equally beige-coloured sheet of paper had informed her that Tex, Silas' father, who had died two months ago in France, had left her something. It was available for collection in the solicitor's office.

A few days later she had made her way over to Inner Temple. The letter had included a map; she was to take the entrance next to Ede & Ravencroft, that venerable manufacturer of English wigs. They had both laughed about it back then. In the juridical heart of London, members of the legal profession were still wearing artificial abundances of hair straight out of Charles Dickens' London with its ubiquitous smog.

When his wife returned (cheerful? excited?), she had shown him the locket here at the table. Red gold, an elegant, embossed rose on its lid. A family heirloom.

She didn't wear it; it was, he presumed, put away in a jewellery box and forgotten.

He forgot it.

Thick brambles were spilling over the outside steps. The light down here had always had an underwater feel to it.

A letter, said Maude, had accompanied the locket. Two letters, to be precise. One new, one old. One from Tex, the other from … A letter from that second summer on Sylt. With a postmark from the day before she died.

He increased his stroke rate, counted, counted.

Rule 11: It is warm.

Brendan was calling out results that took the form of ships' names, punctuated by "fuck" and "bollocks." He was monitoring the route on move-in-real-time.com. They were crossing into the French shipping lane. Far on, thought Charles.

And yet he was disappointed. Here he was, swimming and swimming, and what floated up from his memory? Kitchen scenes from a few weeks back. He could have remembered those easily on dry land. He had been hoping for more, a grander revelation. Or at least some sense of a revelation. Enlightenment was already out of the frame. But change was still a possibility.

Or was it simply like this: everything floated along on the surface?

Like the sea, you perhaps were nothing more than a skin, stroked by the wind, warmed by the sun, covered by darkness at night. Underneath a few fish minded their own business and a whole load of plastic tirelessly waved its plastic arms around. But one thing reigned supreme: emptiness.

He pressed his right calf. Perpendicular, vertical, sparkle, perpendicular, vertical, pain. So this was how it was speaking to him now, his dear Channel. Its teeth were grinding down on Charles' muscles.

Think of Gertrude! It always helped to think of something worse. His calves and brain were cramping, Gertrude Ederle, the first woman to cross the Channel, had been left for the rest of her life with neural malfunctions and tinnitus caused by the constant pounding of the waves. Charles pressed, swore, kicked. When was someone finally going to call for a feed? Magnesium, calcium, ginger, *as many drugs, please, please, as you can*.

Too acidic, shrivelling skin, sea ulcers.

There was black tea too?

Tea. Sugar already in it.

"Lots of milk," said Charles.

Translucently bright, the daytime moon hung low in the sky, well beneath the sun and risen out of nowhere. Later in the afternoon. Was it summertime? It had rained. The wind was blowing. But it was summer nevertheless. It would stay light for hours yet. The waves were fidgeting, as if they were hoping that, after millions of years on the prowl, this very night would be the night for catching the moon and licking it right across its face. Charles licked his lips. The second shipping lane. 500-600 containerships a day, vessels over 1,000-foot long, 80-foot draught, 30,000 tonnage, filled with clothes, cars, molasses, oil. In between all this, 100 conventional ferries, various high-speed ferries, 50-70 yachts, coastguard boats, holiday sailors, warships on practice drills, enormous cruise ships, a few fishing boats, and one or two or three people swimming the Channel, little dots crawling and panting alongside a boat. Braking was out of the question, both for the big ships and for Charles. The former braked horizontally, he went down.

"Ha," said Brendan, "what a joke."

"Ha," said Charles, "what bloody torture."

Ships heading northeast now. Ahead of the French coast they pulled up through the Channel, trying to avoid the Varne sandbank in the middle of the shipping lane. Next to it, the Colbart sandbank set up a run of eddies, with correspondingly strong currents. Hectic traffic merging into the lane, skippers panicking, waves at the bow, transversal swell, also known as the great rendezvous. And then everything was back as before: container ships, luxury transporters, yachts, a cruise ship, ferries, light craft and boats, driftwood, plastic, rubbish and in the middle of all this flotsam – him. How foolish this swimming business was. What a fantastical delusion.

With this thought his cramping leg, at last, had had enough and relaxed.

"Ha?"

"You're not making much progress."

He wasn't swimming briskly enough.

Were they still taking him seriously?

"This will kill me," he shouted up the sheer wall.

Ever more strongly, the swell from the ships was pushing him against the *Henry*. He switched sides.

This!

On a breath, he looked further over to the left. There was no ship to be seen there, just a glittery sea fret. The late afternoon had brought on the haze, his goggles the droplets. The boat's trusty engine was purring, the trusty engine Charles was purring, Sampo, the old boy, was laying his head in his lap. Charles was back in the kitchen. Thanks for that. Is that what he wanted? A crazy levity was reaching out for him. He was a swimming set of cogs, each little cog turning the next with pleasing speed: clockwork, unrest, heart. In his right temple, where his desires and longings had been encircling one another for hours now, a large patch of contentment began to spread. Many people called this fatigue, the second cold phase. He had been warned about her, the most enchanting mermaid of all, the one who sang her captivating song directly in the swimmer's bloodstream, helped along by melatonin, leptin, adenosine.

Blue.

Bl… bl…

Swim, shrieked the boat.

They had got married in April 1981, on a red double decker bus in London. Maude's parents travelled down, Silas' father Tex came to keep Charles' mother company. It was all down to Silas that they had met in the first place, he had been part of their story from the very start. They couldn't not invite him, and if they did, then he had to be Charles' best man. Wasn't he that anyway?

Charles was astonished that Silas accepted without further ado. Admittedly, he did then vanish straight after the afternoon buffet, vanished for almost three decades more or less completely out of their lives (Silas the businessman: elegance, tea, women, travelling. Charles the Chemist: the elegance of particles, research in Germany, Hazel and Maude. Maude: to hell with elegance. New music, concerts, child, husband). But Silas only vanished after having returned, well oiled, from the toilet and staggered towards Charles with a funeral wreath in his arms, embracing him, laying his hands on his shoulders and looking long and hard into his eyes. Totally sober, as Charles well realized.

And do you remember what you saw in those eyes?

Well, what would you call it?

Grief?

Come on, that's cheap. Silas was certainly sad. But not only.

Mockery? That's getting warmer. But only a faint glimmer of mockery. Easily wiped away.

Now it's hotting up: love?

For whom?

Generosity?

Ugh-ugh … how Charles' neck was turning in the water, how his body was wiggling.

She had known for a long time, said Maude, long before the letter from the London solicitor. Abbie had had another relationship alongside Charles. Albeit not with Silas. With Silas' father. A relationship with Tex.

Maude stood up and poured herself a small glass of Sherry.

He thought: When? Abigail a relationship with Tex. He thought: Now?

How ridiculously deluded could you get?

The time period was clearly defined. The same time she was with Charles.

"How?" he asked. He sounded objective. Unchanged, actually.

"In bed, presumably," said Maude. He could tell by her voice that she thought it funny. She was annoying him.

It was quiet in the house. At one point, the wall creaked. The heating was on, a cold May. The tea looked nice in his cup. The white inner rim was reflected in the drink that he had let go cold. On the outside of the cup, a hare was sketched in bold black lines, just the torso and the head. It was wearing the British crown between its ears, in pink.

Abbie had been pregnant with Tex's child, or his, Charles'. The fact that she had had the affair with Tex, said Maude, had tormented her sister. He could surely imagine why. He had known her after all. Abbie loved clarity, liked to determine directions.

The last daffodils were blooming on the slope, a blackbird was singing.

He had known Abbie! Maude didn't say that he had loved her. That stung him. It was true. If only in part.

Just like it was true that Abbie had liked to lay down the rules. She had both attracted and repelled him with this trait.

Both in equal measure. He had recognized himself in her behaviour.

Her sister hadn't wanted to admit to the relationship with Tex, said Maude, not to any of them. She couldn't bear having been so indecisive. It hadn't started in Levain. They had only got to know one another there.

Over the following winter things had developed. Abbie, who travelled to Oxford at the weekend. Tex, who lived in his London apartment and during the week travelled from Charing Cross to Reading. Frequently. Ever more frequently.

Charles said nothing. He could see it all. Tex in tweed with a fur collar. A certain French *je ne sais quoi*, elegant in any case. Inviting Abbie to restaurants, cooking for her, serving her up his meals. Charles remembered having noticed at some point that Abbie meanwhile knew about wine. He personally didn't have much time for *tête-à-têtes*, the lab experiments for his dissertation were in full swing. Of course he was happy when Abbie came to visit, it was only every third or fourth weekend; his head was full of formulas and questions and she provided some distraction by telling him about the films she had seen, apparently a great many, Bergman, Funès, Woody Allen, she owned a video player now too; but he also wasn't wholly unhappy to see her go again.

"She was ashamed to tell you. But also to tell Silas," said Maude. "That it was his father."

So the girls had spoken about it back then?

Maude had known all about it? Had watched her sister go behind his back. That's what he thought: "went behind his back" – and was uncomfortably aware that there had never been any loyalty pact between them. He hadn't been faithful, Abbie had certainly been aware of that, even if he hadn't slept with anyone else. And Abbie herself? He had assumed that he was her only, he had … not thought about it. Considered himself irresistible. And Maude had watched it all.

Could you be hen-pecked without a hen?

That was how it felt.

He was embarrassed. Not because he had been humiliated. He was embarrassed that he had once been so self-assured.

Even though everything that had happened really had floated right by him on the surface. Nothing had been hidden. He just hadn't seen it for a long time. And then, when he did know about it, he had chosen immediately to forget it.

"Poor Abs," said Maude. And poured him a Sherry too.

They sat in silence. The male blackbird on the jasmine shrub jerked his head a couple of times. The man-sized fridge sprang into action.

How ridiculous. His girlfriend and that old guy! Although, Tex had been in his mid-forties when they stayed with him in Levain. Charles had no difficulty now in imagining a forty-year-old man with a twenty-year-old woman. This was also not helpful.

Only then did he realize: when Maude, as she had just said, already knew about the relationship long before Tex's letter, how could she ever have believed his lie about Abbie sleeping with Silas?

There it lay, floating along the top. You just had to join the dots.

Maude made scant attempt at hiding her satisfied smile.

For her, his old letter had mattered in a different way. Perhaps, she said, he might like to read the end of it again, the very last lines.

Ever its nose in front, the ship ahead of him rose and fell with the waves. The waves carried the ship up and down, commanding their own path forward. Theirs was a different path to the ship, a different path to Charles. And each individual wave also took its own individual course. The sky rose and fell and spun. Charles retched, nothing came.

Look, said Brendan, if he didn't pick up the pace right away he would take him out. It was coming up for six.

Waves pounding in his head, the rest a glassy emptiness. Was that a giggle he just heard? Nonsense. It was just the grinding mill all around.

Charles waved to the pilot to signal intent. His hand looked like a foreign object as it slid back into the water. Waxy and white, almost totally wrinkle-free once more.

Throbbing, the pulse in his throat. Backwards and forwards the clouds were shoving each other, falling into a heap and pulling away from one another again, clumps of cotton wool scattering in all directions.

"Are you still listening?" Now she was finally going to tell him what was really on her mind. It concerned them both.

He looked at her.

"Yes," she said, "us." But Silas in the first instance.

Tex had left her the locket to thank her for not saying anything to Silas. She had bluffed. Just now! Told a white lie. In truth, she didn't find out about Abbie's affair with Silas' father until after Abbie's death. Over a decade later. Abbie had only said she was pregnant. And Charles was the father. The idea that there might be someone else in Abbie's life was only conjecture on her part, as her sister. Yes, she as good as knew it. Suspected Tex. It was hardly difficult to figure out.

He groaned but had sufficient presence of mind only to do so inwardly. There it was again, Maude's incredible ability to bring clarity to the table and then immediately destroy it.

A gifted musician. She would set the tone, tease it out, make a melody. And then another would follow naturally on, interweave with the first.

Nothing was straightforward with her. Quite the opposite of him, with his formulas, test-tube reactions, mathematical equations full of =.

He must have looked pained or doubtful, it was one of those moments in a marriage (or after a marriage) where you didn't think you were letting anything slip, but the other person saw it nonetheless (whatever they thought it might be), felt annoyed or touched (in spite of themselves), only that this time Maude remained factual. "Come on!"

Tex. Wasn't this obvious? He had only to consider how often Abbie had travelled to London. Instead of Oxford. And often enough travelled on from there too. Honestly, what had he been thinking?

Nothing?

Not even the franc notes in her purse had struck him as odd. But surely he must have seen them?

Maude sighed. She didn't find out for sure until years later in Levain-le-Bain. On her second visit to the Cevennes, when she was there with Hazel and him, Tex had told her about his affair with Abbie.

"Abbie thought it was yours. All the same, Tex had offered her every support. He was prepared to move back to England, take care of the child, irrespective of the father. She rejected it all. She wanted you."

He couldn't help it: he was flattered. Fortunately, probably even Maude couldn't spot that. Just to be safe, he lowered his gaze and drank a sip of tea. Cold and sweet.

The second visit to Tex's house, Charles did the calculations quickly in his head, was fifteen years ago. Perhaps a little more.

"You never told me about Tex … about his involvement. Not a word," he said.

She considered him as if he were the hare on the cup. A hare with a carrot, and she were wondering whether she should leave him to nibble away or lure him further down the garden path.

"Well," he said hastily, "now we're quits."

He had written a letter sowing doubts about Silas that he himself had only half believed; she had kept Tex's confession from him. Each had guarded their own secret.

His letter of lies. No. His love-letter of lies. His love-letter. With an emergency lie.

"Is that so?" she said.

He swallowed.

Maude sounded sure of herself. Almost triumphant. Was she keeping something in her back pocket? Had she hatched one of those plans that only women can make, terrifyingly opaque, always thinking around the chips on people's shoulders that he, Charles, hadn't even noticed they had? He thought about Tex.

He swam.

And thought about Tex. There had been something else. Tex, relaxed, tanned. That second visit in Levain. Footsteps, something warm. Tex's feet in sandals. The ground, a piece of bacon, dropped, scrambled egg next to it, hot dripping oil. The next word was almost on his – swollen from the salt water – tongue. He almost had it.

"Mister C!"

Charles' gaze twitched upwards.

"7.00 p.m. Well done!" said his man with the shining eyes.

Two very similar looking ferries dotted the horizon like a constellation in the sky. Cedric confirmed: Charles had made progress. Arrival perhaps, with a bit of luck, around two.

He felt his joy in a lessening of pain in his neck: unexpectedly good time made on the water.

He was ready! There was just this impenetrable knot of effort and salt sitting in the middle of his throat. Carbohydrates for his liver, or else his body would revert to burning fat, a final flare up that would consume all the oxygen in his blood in one last panic. Or had he already reached that stage?

He shouted something in the direction of the ship.

Brendan's hands formed a funnel at Brendan's mouth. They were staggeringly big.

And yet only Charles' mouth was growing bigger! Not a single word that the pilot shouted made it to him. Instead he found himself thinking: that thing Brendan had said about darkness. That every person, on the inside, was thick, soft darkness.

Food? Oh. He was already swimming again. He was wonderfully deaf. And no giant hand ploughed through the air, no angry ship's captain grabbed him by the neck and pulled him out. So he could.

His body was dark, it wasn't soft. Inside, he roiled.

For the entire winter he had trained on the Isis. Rubbed himself down afterwards, wrapped himself up, sat on a park bench drinking tea from a thermos flask with shaking fingers. Behind the stiff, skeletal trees of the early morning lay Merton Field, it too covered in a milky-white hoar-frost from the previous night. Dark patches formed where the frost was melting; something in all this resembled Charles' life, he didn't know what, he just knew it did.

In the bare, glittering trees the indigenous crows, black as peat, tore their beaks open wide; the ancestors of the ancestors of these crows yanked their eyes open wide – they sat in the plane-trees on St. Giles at five in the morning, still dark, and snatched after dreams, food, and ego.

After Maude had, while still at the solicitor's, read Abbie's letter to Tex that was post-marked from Sylt on the 22 August 1978 and "not a farewell letter," she had told Silas that he, Charles, was the one who had sown discord between them in the following autumn. Silas didn't say much. Shrugged his shoulders. It had been obvious. Who else!

Maude had subsequently apologized to Silas. For having been so petty back then. She had distrusted him too rashly on reading Charles' lines.

"But," said Maude, "Silas generously dismissed it."

Charles looked at her. She was sitting very upright, facing him. A red hue had flushed over her cheeks, he didn't think that was from the Sherry.

Silas had said she may well have had good reasons for her reservations in 1978, but only half realized them herself back then. Reliability, he remembered all too well, had not been his strong suit. London had turned into a kind of airport for him, he needed to see more of the world and would have headed off at some point anyway. Without her. He loved music as a hobby, for her it was a vocation. What would she have done as a concert pianist in Darjeeling, on the Huang Shan slopes in Eastern China, or on the high plateau around Nuwara Eliya in Southern Sri Lanka, where he spent years visiting tea plantations and striking business deals?

These words, she said, had brought back to her the tenderness between them when it had come to a no. It hadn't been just the music but also Maude's parents that had made her want to stay in Europe. It had been the right decision, and sad; Silas and she had mutually agreed to part ways.

"Caused by your letter?" Mockery flashed in her eyes. Didn't he know he had a tendency to dramatize. To overplay his own importance. She hadn't made up her mind yet as to which of these traits were more damning. His letter had been a trigger, yes. They had taken what he said seriously. After all, he was their best friend. And how about a bit of generosity of spirit – now, from him?

She took a piece of shortbread, but only nibbled at it with her front teeth. Neither spoke for a while.

Not even the dog was there, he had been taken out by a professional dog-walker to some park or other, in a whole pack of dogs. Maude's left knee hurt. Neither of them was getting any younger. That's what they always said, no, always had said, whenever one of those age-related niggles with a bone or a tendon reared its head. And if it had been possible, he thought to himself now on that kitchen chair, would she have beamed herself back to autumn 1978? And decided differently? He wouldn't. He wouldn't have decided anything differently.

"Are you listening, Charlie? There's … there's something else."

Their friend didn't suspect, said Maude, that the relationship levelled at him really had existed, only with his father instead of him. After he broke up with Maude, Silas had fled to Levain-le-Bain and poured his heart out to Tex. Tex, however, either couldn't bring himself to come clean or didn't believe it was necessary. He had not admitted to his son, who sat before him wallowing in the complexities of life, or rather, his love-life, that he, his old man, might have fathered another child. With the sister of his son's girlfriend. Who was also the girlfriend of this son's best friend.

No, that didn't sound good. That sounded uncomfortable, and it was. So Tex had kept quiet and certainly hadn't mustered the courage to dig it all back up shortly before his death.

"And?" said Charles.

Tex! He was just what he needed now. Tex with his French face and American figure. Tex, far too good-looking, far too casual, far too full of life to be walking around in theirs. Twice he had been to this man's stone castle in the south of France, once as a young man and then more or less by accident many years later, with Hazel and Maude. Not even in stature had he ever had a chance of keeping up with Silas' father.

"Admit it, he was moaning because he lost you as his daughter-in-law, because the two of you, you and his son, would have been the perfect couple."

Maude looked distinctly uncomfortable. It almost made him laugh. How complicated people were. Everyone was always vying for their own position, trying to get ahead of the pack and offload their problems on to others.

The truth hit him like a bolt. "Silas never said that he *hadn't* slept with Abbie, right?"

Now he really was laughing, even if only inwardly and primarily in surprise. How many swimming camps had he and Silas attended together? How many rooms had they shared with each other? And how often had Charles waited outside the door? Trying not to hear anything?

Wouldn't Maude have had to assume right from the start the thing that he was only starting to realize just now: that Abbie, flexible Abbie, actually probably had slept with Silas? Quite apart from the fact that she was also going to bed with the father of Maude's boyfriend, not to mention Charles, who was her official boyfriend. While Maude, who had thought herself queen bee, the focal point, more desirable than her sister, was now the naïve, reserved, and, for all her beauty, undeniably less successful of the two?

She said she had advised Tex to let the matter rest. Tex had immediately shot back at her: does love have its time?

Of course, she had replied. She still thought so today. "Its time. And sometimes two. And …" said Maude. Maude with flushed cheeks and a quiet voice.

Charles stood up and went to the kitchen window. So that was what this was about: that one love could have two times. And two loves … one time. He was surprised the tiles weren't too cold for Maude's bare feet. Here, by the door out to the garden steps, a draught was coming through all the cracks. The packet of shortbread lay open in front of him, furtively he put half a biscuit in his mouth.

After a while he turned back to face Maude. She had also stood up, was leaning with her bottom against the table-top.

She would lay it all out for him now, no more secrets. In that week in August in Levain, when Tex had told her about his relationship with Abbie and then about Silas (never did he marry), she decided to stick with what she had. "Call it the soft option if you want." Or being smart. It meant she could look herself in the mirror. She had had a good life. And had sided with the the good stuff in life. A daughter who made her happy. Who was happy with her father. "And with whom I was happy, most of the time." She would gladly repeat it: in Levain, she had sided with what was already there, the world at Charles' side.

He said nothing.

"You know what I found out in Abbie's final lines."

Did he wish the earth might swallow him up? It had already done so. Abbie hadn't just told him she was pregnant on that evening on Sylt, she had also indicated that there had been someone else on occasion. Said he should know everything. That she wanted to put an end to the affairs now. Start afresh, with him. She had produced her diary and talked him through the dates. The result was clear: it had to be his child. He hadn't disagreed. He knew as well as her when it had happened.

"She wrote," continued Maude, "that you listened carefully to her, looked at her, let her finish and thanked her clearly and calmly. Then you burst out laughing. A nice, long laugh, not too quiet, not too loud. Laughter that was almost heart-warming. But only in as much as hearing someone laugh with relief can be heart-warming."

He was back in the room in Rantum. On the windowsill lay a few grotesquely shaped, washed-up roots. Behind the glass pane sand, clumpy grass, a piece of the Hindenburg Dam only recognisable to those who already knew what it was supposed to be. A glass of apple juice in hand, they sat on the floor facing each other. Abbie drank and stretched her feet out towards him. He saw her face in front of him, her big nose, her forehead minus the cowlick, her light, bright curls framing her features. She was talking, he let her get it all out, he waited, and when nothing more came he said adieu, ciao, goodbye, and started laughing. He was irate. His fury took him by surprise. She just looked at him, not reproachfully, not even questioningly. It was more an empty look, her face seemed so open and so vulnerable that it was as if his reaction might have finished off or emptied something in her for ever, and, for just a few seconds, this changed state of affairs was voiding all possible expression.

She even repeated her question.

"Charley?"

As if she were giving him a second chance.

Thanks and get lost. He remembered it all too clearly. He had said it twice. And pushed Abbie and the child inside her out of the room. Wasn't somebody else looking after her now?

Practical Tex! Idiotic Tex.

He had been irate – and confused.

And so he had laughed at her. Because that too was a face of love when you were in denial?

Maude took two rash steps towards him: "You'll hear me out!"

She had told him everything today entirely off her own bat. Against Tex's explicit wishes. So now all the cards were on the table. Including the fact that Silas didn't know everything about his father's life. And didn't need to.

All of a sudden she looked tense. Her hair was messed up, silver streaks ran through the brown.

"Have you apologized to him? Or to me? Would you just do something, you … you teaspoon!"

She turned her head away from him.

Only one thing was turning over in his head: that sentence "One love, two times." It had changed into "two loves, one time," but now it was changing back again. Wasn't this a particular figure in music? This kind of swapping? He couldn't think what it was called. But Maude didn't want to swap her men. She wanted to add them together.

Paws trotted down the cellar staircase, a snout prized open the kitchen door, a snout pressed itself into his hand. Sampo danced and whimpered delightedly between his legs; the creature was so happy, it was almost contagious.

Maude and "her men."

Charles stroked Sampo's head. Long-haired, soft, and doggy warm. This helped him think. Helped him regain his poise.

He pulled himself forwards. The afternoon was never-ending. "The vastness of the salt world," said something in his head. Something else giggled. It was loud enough *at* sea, never mind being *in* it. The chugging of the engine, the swirling of the air, the breaking and pounding of the waves. Every bone was vibrating, bending, turning to mush. His head was blethering, his sinews were singing, or was that the fish, there must be some, but none that his eyes could make out. You didn't realize what you had until you had lost everything. How trivial.

And what if you could feel it, what was it then?

The organs in his chest seemed to have melted into a single dark, tough block, he was straining on it with every movement.

A kind of salt frost had formed on his eyelids, his eyes were shrinking by the minute and the layer of grease in his ears acted like wax. Now, after twelve hours in the water – it took him a while to do the maths and even then he wasn't sure he had got it right –, now his ears were opening again, and he could hear himself swimming. Every fibre in his body was stretching and the depths were no longer pulling him down; they were reaching up to him. They were carrying him, touching him. He was splashing about in them.

So he knew that the third, the most dangerous part of his attempt, had begun. It was the part where you swam through yourself.

Hazel, all of ten years old, on the back of a donkey, her face level with his, pointed it out to him: "There!"

Above the treetops.

Olives, plane-trees and other trees with thick, deep-green leaves whose names he didn't know lined the path, interspersed with thorny undergrowth that yielded bursts of wild cumin and small, white-headed roses. Bathed in dappled-leaf light, the path, about half-way up the hillside, wound its way northwards. A small stream ran through the valley with fields and groves of walnut trees nestling along its banks. Coming on in the village that appeared around the next bend in the path the first lights twinkled like promises through the dark trees of the slope. Charles had to stride with purpose, the donkey carrying his daughter was keen to get home.

"Up there, look!"

It was a cloud.

Flying backwards.

"You wouldn't see anything without me!" said Hazel.

At home in Levain, Tex explained that an individual cloud moving backwards was an unusual but known meteorological phenomenon of the area. Certain inverse weather conditions at the foot of the Cevennes created thin, strong jets of air. If these met with winds blowing from the sea they could shoot out in a tunnel of air and would funnel along in front of themselves anything they encountered. Birds of prey took pleasure in letting themselves be carried off on this stream for a time, then peeled away to the side and flew on the main wind, against the jet in the tunnel, only to be flung back by the jet for a second and a third time to the starting point of their adventure. Skiing, with a wind-lift and a horizontal slope, said Tex, a local sport for birds.

A parasite had done for all the silkworms. Tex said he had in any case had enough of the strange teeming mass and decided to change over to something that you were at least allowed to touch. He was repairing the inside mechanisms of wind instruments and antique clocks. For the first time, Charles had a common point of interest with the father of his lost friend. Unexpectedly the German technical term for the driver mechanism behind the hands on a clock popped into his head: *Unruhe*. And each little piece really did pulsate under Tex's hands like a heart.

Charles put Hazel to bed. When he joined the host and Maude in the living room, a lump of wood as thick as an arm was crackling in the open hearth, traditional English-style. He wondered what Silas looked like these days, but Tex wasn't the sort of person to put photos on the mantlepiece. It had felt a bit awkward, just turning up here after so many years had passed. Montezuma's Revenge had afflicted Hazel so badly on the return from their holiday in Spain that the girl had refused to travel any further. In the car Charles learned that his wife had remained in touch with Tex, or rather, that Tex had not let the contact with Abbie's sister fall away. He had agreed to make a stop in Levain, seeing as it almost lay along the route, until Hazel felt better, and Tex had turned out to be such an enthusiastic host that they were finding it almost impossible to leave. On this evening, however, the man was almost monosyllabic and after not very long he excused himself. The oldest donkey here was him, he said, or at any rate he was as exhausted as one, apologies, but he really must head to bed. Maude, her hair and cheeks shining, looked silently into the flames and twiddled a pen between her fingers.

Tex had honoured the couple with his old four-poster bed, where an hour later they lay in a tranquil pool of sweat and satisfaction, the final rays of the sunset still flickering between the branches of the chestnut tree. Their dog, Sampo's ancestor, was searching for his flying evening desert; he nuzzled at Charles and they laughed at the animal who believed his master provided everything in the world, including flies.

Maude said, yes, she did sometimes think about Silas. At home too. She had spoken with Tex about his son before Charles had joined them. And had got the impression Silas wasn't doing badly, she laughed shyly. But actually, these days she found herself thinking less about Silas and more about her sister. Didn't Hazel look a bit like Abbie, Maude asked with a second laugh. Later, Charles would often remember this when he found himself looking at his daughter, anxiously searching for traces of the lost Abbie, but, to his relief, only ever finding Maude.

Tex was already standing at the stove when Charles came down shortly after sunrise the following morning.

"Oh, it's you."

"Disappointed?"

"Quite the opposite, Charles, quite the opposite."

As if to underscore what he had just said, Tex, looking unashamedly the man of the house as he stood, tanned and barefoot, in his casual t-shirt and checked shorts, turned up the gas under the frying pan. It was one of those real, cast-iron ones that Charles had wanted to buy for a long time. Tex added two extra eggs to the portion that was already cooking, four slices of bacon. They found themselves talking about Hazel, school, Maude's music. No brother or sister for the girl? Who didn't have any cousins either, right? Wasn't Hazel a little lonely?

No, she was very happy in Germany, heaps of friends.

Charles talked away. The night with Maude had been … more electric than usual, fervent, deep. She had called it "the unfamiliar bed," he had gladly followed her lead, felt how she was looking for him or looking for something different in him to usual, and he tried to answer her until he really was holding her, both inside and out.

Now that he started thinking about it in Tex's kitchen, the expedition with Hazel and the night that had just passed started to blend into one another; perhaps it was the tiredness, but for a few moments it was as if he were seeing his family and himself from the outside. There they were, swimming in their shared life. It felt nice, a bubble full of afternoon sunshine and movement, the child, who was just about still a child and smelled of childhood, her warmth, her trust, trotting along beside him. And then the river, its lights, and how they headed back to Maude who was waiting for them. Did you only ever see happiness in hindsight? Surely there were exceptions. Occasionally it had flashed up when they were in the thick of it, and Charles was amazed by the radiant life they had as a family of three. Maude had accompanied him to Germany, she taught Music and English, called herself a digital pioneer, was proud of it. Hazel became as German as she was English, teemed with stories, and they got her Sampo the First for afternoons without playmates. When Charles returned home the creature would come bounding over to him, Hazel was in her room on the first floor or he could hear her shrieking in the garden with her friends, Maude was playing piano, ringing the school, the plumber, or friends *at home*, which meant in *English*. The millennium came and went, new buildings kept shooting up in London, increasingly the city seemed foreign to him. They intended to go there more frequently but never got round to it. In the kitchen, the used cups piled up over the course of the day (and from the day before, if Charles hadn't tidied them away), the dirty dishes. Sometimes Maude and Hazel sang for him while he was washing up or was acting the dustbin for them (the classic male hero role at the table on both sides of the Channel). Hazel was one and half when he fell down the stairs with her on a night feed. It was painful enough, bruises and a bang to the hip, but he was extremely pleased with himself: instead of protecting himself, he had held the child up high. His instincts seemed sound. From then on, he trusted himself to be a father. Even though he was only allowed to sing in the shower, under the noise of the water, and this still didn't stop his wife and child banging on the door and running off shouting.

Sometimes he saw Abigail, pictured in his memory or projected into one of his thoughts. He saw how things might have been had she lived, and he missed her as someone who had been close to all three of them. His grief for her had become an abstract quantity, only occasionally, perhaps once a year and then in a dream, did he really miss her. When that happened, it was like he had momentarily passed over into the reverse of another life, a soft expanse that had nearly wholly dissipated. Perhaps he shouldn't overlook this void when he was considering everything he had, and there, in Tex's kitchen, he wanted nothing more for himself than for his life to continue as it was. Maude's electricity, her body, her music that he had heard right from the very first time he set eyes on her, or as good as, in that first week on Sylt, coursed through him.

Abbie's death had united Charles and Maude in a new way that was no less intense or meaningful. They shared her memory and after Maude's visit to Oxford they had found a way of offering mutual support. Charles was unquestionably a member of the family, quite different to how Silas could be or might ever have wanted to be. Maude's comparative reticence, which broke when she played piano, further attracted him. Maybe his wife was sometimes difficult. Buried in old scores, lost for hours every day in a world of notes that she didn't share with him. And then again, courting, demanding, not relenting, he would reach a physical closeness with her where instinctive movements and rhythms determined everything, and there was no inside or outside any more. Maude didn't hold back there either.

Tex boxed him on the shoulder, "Hey, are you asleep on your feet?," and steered him to the dining table. "At least you're out of the way over here."

He was happy to sit down. It was nice to be served coffee, breathe in the aroma of bacon, and -- wasn't that the whole point of still being on holiday? -- not think about anything.

The gas flame was licking up to the rim of the pan. Must be some kind of turbo-fry, a French trick, he'd remember that. He spent some time piecing together his schoolboy French with the local paper that was lying on the table. Afterwards he couldn't say why, he raised his head at just that moment, a few minutes later. Tex, who in his bare feet had silently come up beside him, angled the pan while lifting his serving arm, as if about to swim front crawl. From high above and at an almighty speed, the iron came whistling through the air, a glowing, flat cap with an equally glowing rim, sharp as a knife, heading straight for Charles. Eggs and bacon flew through the air, the pan hissed just past Charles, who ducked but still felt the heat burning his neck and right arm. A thump on the tabletop, fat spraying in all directions.

Tex swore. Charles thought to hear a "slipped...," "'pologies." Hot oil dripped onto the floor, some of the eggs and bacon were on the ground, some had been scattered over the table.

"Bad habit," muttered Tex, picking up the pan, turning it over and inspecting it. The edge of the table had a significant notch.

This bloody living alone, said Tex, always made him serve like that.

And, with a glance over at Charles and a laugh that rang in Charles' ears, he threw the hot, heavy utensil from where he stood into the sink ten feet away.

A precision aim! The water in the sink hissed and a plume of steam rose up.

Only later in the bathroom did Charles see the singed patch next to his temple. It had smelled of burned hair, burned skin. He could already sense the blister forming when he was clearing the table, but he hadn't wanted to make a fuss. The pan had ripped past his head.

At the last second he had flinched to one side.

Maude was standing in her nightdress at the kitchen table when they told her. How daft of Charles to offer up his skull, as it were, to the pan! Just as Tex was trying to dish up the breakfast sizzling in hot oil. So that he almost would have hit him.

Sleepyhead Charley!

Together they laughed it off.

Tex pulling his head out of the noose.

They left that same afternoon. It was easy, everyone seemed to think it was time.

"… very tired. Your legs are sinking."

"…"

"Your legs are going down."

Brendan, faded out.

"Ha?"

"You've got to swim."

"You've got to go faster."

"…"

"That waaaay?" He sounded like a crow with a cough. He had to admit it. Pretty scratchy. Practically clanking.

"If you go on like this it will be twenty-three hours."

" — "

"I'm telling you the truth."

"Ha?"

"The truth!"

For a few seconds, the residual strength in his arms and the torque of the waves worked in unison rather than competition. An empty space opened up around him, through which a few remnants of his brain, over-sweetened from exertion, floated. If he carried on swimming so slowly he would need twenty-three hours for the crossing. The truth? He couldn't feel anything anymore. Everything was pleasant. As long as truth lay in the hands of his magical pilot he didn't need to grapple with it.

In the water, torsos and souls were floating all around.

They had as good as passed the French shipping lane. The *Henry*'s headlights flickered on; the water ahead of the bow transformed, as if it were reliable and obedient, into a coherent mass of greenish white. Early evening, warm yellow rays of sunlight were running ahead of the weather that Brendan claimed to have talked about just now – on a day like today? – running away from it and yet presumably right into it too. Like erect, thin spirits, the mist banks were rolling in.

Yet again, too much was happening.

The weather was seeking to destroy the sea. It was swallowing it up. While the Channel hid itself in the white mist, playing at being a sky whose transparent, watery tufts and threads melted away in a matter of seconds into the saltier element, the southerly firmament above was swelling to an almighty arch. Over a greasy slick of oil cannisters, decaying moss and grassroots-green floated a poisonous crystal yellow. All around Charles, ever more opaque, white banks of mist were settling down on the crests of the Channel with a kind of smiling delight. The waves, quasi-cropped, were now scurrying along underneath the new, tufty veils; Charles was sure he could hear a quiet panting here and there, as if the hunters were now hunting themselves.

The person who was supposed to be swimming between the waves and the cloud banks sucked on his feeding slime and wished that this forecast fog might herald the end of everything else too. If the world was going to dissolve into a milky dampness, couldn't pain and torment please follow suit? Half empty? Half full? Enough. Charles would paddle over to the *Henry*, touch the boat, everything would be over.

"Ah," said his master of the crossing, "this is it."

They had discussed it in the pub, how everyone had to crawl their own way through their crises, get a grip on themselves again.

Themselves or someone else, thought Charles.

Such thoughts meanwhile came easily. God, along with Jesus, was sitting in his armpits. From there, he needled. Master Brendan, the glorious seeker of paradise who had left his men to camp on the back of a whale while he stayed nice and safe on his boat, was squatting on Charles' top vertebra, executing enthusiastic pirouettes and plaguing every muscle and nerve fibre in Charles' back. Brendan, the pilot, was trying to tell his distinctly brow-beaten customer something about candyfloss threads that had spun their way down into watery troughs. The little swimming fella waved him off.

He had practiced crossing in the dark. But not maintaining direction in the fog. He wouldn't be the first to be swallowed unceremoniously by the Channel.

A passenger ferry drew astonishingly near. The French coast had to be close; real now – and close. Even the ferry was going slowly, Charles heard an on-board message, could see each window. People looking out from the ship's decks wouldn't be able to discern a swimmer in the soup of fog. He had become invisible, a ghost.

The ghost crawled his way through milk and saw the travellers sitting in their bright, warm house.

With astonishing speed it drew away under the first stars.

It gave him strength to know he was outside and hidden and, at the same time, he could see that big home, glowing, boxy and warm, travelling over the cushion of water. If you saved yourself, did you also save those around you? Obediently Mr C. Aquarius duck-dived under, lifting his bottom and wriggling under the hand of the ship's pilot. Brendan clipped a pair of light sticks to his trunks.

Neon green this time.

"You're fighting!" said the pilot. This they respected. So they would give him a chance. The fog bank must be small, as otherwise the helmsman on the ferry would have warned them.

He was allowed to continue! Go on.

She was at the helm, Cedric was supervising but let her take the wheel; this way, he could be the teacher for once (she didn't begrudge him this). Voices from the deck of the *Spirit of Britain* reached over to them. But even faster than the voices faded, the entire ship disappeared into the thick pea soup. An unanticipated sense of agreement, appropriateness even, took hold of Matilda as her sight was limited to the instruments in the cabin. It was as if the earth were using this weather to return to a more original form. Left to its own devices, it was amusing itself as in times of old, when no warm-blooded creatures disturbed it, only plants grew, insects buzzed, and the sun passed over it all. Nothing was bad or good; wind, cloud, hurricane – phenomena, nameless, for an age and ever again, for eternity. It was enough to drown for. With the stern light of the *Spirit* every last limitation vanished.

Only momentarily and a little anxiously did Matilda look to the left. Their tiddler! How it glowed and kicked.

The waves swelled triumphantly, as if they might break into a victory march at any moment. Could they sense how alone Charles was, thanks to the fog? The agate-green was fading. Grey. He noticed the water at the edges of his arms, but oddly they didn't accord with the edges he could see. For seconds (?), minutes (?) he watched himself from the outside. He almost forgot to swim. In this water-milk - or should he say sky-milk? the individual words no longer made any difference now – even his own movement might as well be made up.

The murky weather swallowed Charles' hand at the end of his outstretched arm. His breaststroke started behind his hands. He only resorted to that movement to relieve his legs. His hands were numb. His thinking started in front of his forehead.

Be afraid!

Don't be afraid!

Now, don't be afraid of being afraid.

He wasn't anything. He was calmness incarnate. And he knew why. It made him laugh. An airless laugh. You had to be really knackered to manage this; he could still hear it, he heard it distinctly. Swimming in a fog without fear.

He had lived too safely and now he was sick of it. But only since he'd lost all safety anyway. He laughed. How honest was that! What a manoeuvre. He was swimming away from his own desire and at the same time swimming ever deeper into it. The darkness of the encroaching summer's night was hardly necessary for such a feat. The fog had already left him to his own devices. All gone, the others, all gone the theatrical stage. At least, the stage he had shared with people. The sea must still be there. It was hanging out of its own waves like the tongue of a panting dog. He quite liked that: him too.

Images rose up in his mind: King's Cross, tall, white, empty of trains, pure architecture, a boy in trousers and a t-shirt, a tall, old man next to him. A wizard's cloak, long beard.

"Tell me one last thing," said Harry. "Is this real? Or has this been happening inside my head?"

"Of course it is happening inside your head, Harry, but why on earth should that mean that it is not real?"

He had seen the last of the Potter films with Hazel. The apprentice wizard, just killed by Lord Voldemort, picked himself back up off the ground next to a bench, sharp sighted now, no glasses. The most senior wizard of all, headteacher Dumbledore, dead for a year, expression serene, was talking to him about arrivals, departures and decisions. A worm of a person, neither an embryo nor an adult, writhed under the bench.

Charles, an adult and, as far as the parts of his body went that were still warm, an oxygenated worm, breathed the damp that was now engulfing him above water too. Far away from all the headlights, just for him, a last fleck of blue fluttered for a heartbeat on a wave, like two fine wings. The violet blue of Silas' eyes. He reached out for it, closed his fingers around it, pressed. What Maude had confided in him in the kitchen came back to him, "I've told you everything. And when you finally figure out why…"

Maude hadn't pointed a gun at his heart. Oh no, just love and memories, and told him that the door was still open, but not for much longer. He would have to decide.

She had been trying to effect an about-turn in his feelings for Silas. He, Charles, was furious with the guy. She, Maude, wanted the three of them to make it work. He, Charles, felt inferior to Silas: the guy had pinched back his wife. That's how it looked. And that's how it felt most of the time too. And now she was trying to give him strength, that was why she had showed him Silas' weakness. Silas' father hadn't told him the whole truth. He, Charles, could let slip the rest. Maybe not a dramatic revelation anymore, not after so many years, but a careful, painful correction nevertheless. Maude, meanwhile, really wasn't bothered by it. He saw this quite clearly now. It didn't matter one bit to her whether he spilled Tex's secret or not. Maude was aiming for right now – she was trying to bore a hair's breadth of a tunnel into the very inner workings of Charles. Ah, that was what "knowing someone for a long time" meant. "Being really close." That you could do that. And tried. And wanted to try.

And you, for your part, let it happen.

Because she had touched him. Neither his anger with Silas nor his desire to get rid of him had disappeared. But the other, old Silas had re-emerged in Charles' inner world: the friend. He wasn't sorry he had written the letter, love versus friendship, they just didn't equate, he was still quite sure of that. Back then, Charles had ended the friendship with Silas, or at least his loyalty to him. He had hardened himself against his old companion in order to do so.

And then Maude showed him Silas' weak spot. He didn't just see it, he sensed it. And he softened.

Because Maude had told him something Silas didn't know.

Something where Silas was kind of innocent. Innocent like you might say of a child.

Silas who, of the four of them, had always least understood the game that was being played.

Abbie and Maude, Silas and Charles.

Two sisters and two brothers, nearly. Something of that old, unspoken closeness to his childhood friend was coming back. And, with that, something of that old, invincible group of four.

He took his time working this out. He was treading icy water, after all. He was probably always slow with things like this. Now he realized. This wasn't about Silas, it was about the three-four of them.

The three and the four of them, he told himself. "Three," left stroke, "four," right stroke.

It wasn't just that his wife knew him; she really wanted him back. Not the same as before, fair enough, but she wasn't pushing him away. How easily he glided now, thinking this. Maude was composing a melody with three living instruments and a fourth, played by the wind. She perceived the borders between people differently now, and she had shared her thoughts with him. Music was a whole, each instrument responding to the others. Anyone could hear this. But almost no one knew what actually made the sound. It happened in the rests. When you heard nothing. These so-called rests were never empty, quite the opposite, and it was from this wealth of resonance that surpassed all control and escaped your ear, it was from this that the actual music was made.

"Don't be such a prig," she had said, "there's no way you're such a prig about marriage."

And the letter on the fridge? The scales fell from his eyes. It hadn't been hanging there because of his lie about Abbie. Maude had wanted to remind him of something else: the end. *If you need me, Maude: I'm here for you. And will be, whatever happens.*

Water mountains, semi-visible, semi-submerged, were pressing onwards. It came as a surprise to him that waves grew in the fog. Thick with damp, the air seemed to draw them on and force them up. It was logical that Charles couldn't see the *Henry*. But, with horror, he realized that he also couldn't hear her anymore either.

Was he frightened now after all? Has this brought him back to life? If he, the human, began imagining frames and painting them into the white in front of him, the fog yielded an angular world. He could layer box upon box inside each another. That way everything hung together again, if only in his human head. Otherwise, his heart was pounding and something like agitation was shooting through his veins. He improved his box formation.

And so the weather was not entirely formless.

The adrenaline was still coming in spurts, albeit only in the smallest of doses, through his stiff veins. Without the *Henry* he would be lost. He felt incredibly calm for all that. It was as if everything were affecting him only in the abstract.

If they didn't find him again, here in this salt soup, he could write off the crossing. Even if he made it to the beach on his own.

Which was doubtful.

To be really scared, to panic, you needed energy.

His fear came and went in spurts that lasted only seconds. He experienced it and at the same time he watched himself going through it. The exhaustion was splitting him in two. How could all this be happening to him? His bones were rattling. But he had stopped shivering a long time ago.

His joy in what he had just realized carried him further. It too was form. Maude had reflected and then come up with this solution: she had appealed to his soft nature.

Perhaps also just his sentimentality.

Beyond all coordinates, a sharp, grandiose picture of his situation flashed before his eyes: his head sticking up into the vast desert of fog, and this in turn floating on the much larger, curved expanse of the sea.

The head-sphere reflected the lights from the *Henry*. That was the optimistic version.

The less optimistic one: The spherical head slipping away, abandoned and alone, over the slate-coloured, foggy surface of the sea. As small as the Lego head from a merchild's toybox.

No one would ever find it again.

Pink! Yellow! Pink!

Ten feet above water. He saw it distinctly. Gradually something solid, white came to the fore. Charles waved euphorically. Euphorically he grinned at the boat's hull.

Pink-yellow grinned back through the wheel-house.

Brendan was hanging over the railing of the deck starboard side, Cedric portside. They were still looking for him. Even though they had found him. Or he them. Now, thought Charles, that this has ended well, he would, reassuringly foolish, yes indeed, also be able to pull himself, no pain, no torment, through the rest of the Channel!

The *Henry* heaved to. Brendan wanted to attach a fresh pair of light sticks. The green ones were shite. Stayed up nice and straight but had no glow at all.

As did the thing. The Charles. Trunks, goggles, ice-cold flesh.

The ship's captain looked at him with a sharpness that pierced his heart.

"What's up?"

His heart fluttered. Orange sticks now, like the first ones.

Instantly, joy washed over him. Instantly, his whole situation became as clear as if a hand had just wiped the air.

He was free. He could decide. The Channel had brought him to a state where the obfuscating film that had settled over everything he encountered simply dissolved. It was as if a new dimension were bearing down on him. It grabbed him by the scruff of the neck. What he thought-knew-felt (until right now he hadn't known anything) descended upon him and enveloped him from all sides. It seemed as if he were floating in a lion's mouth. It was black, albeit not totally, this lion's mouth with serried white teeth and lion's stink, half open, and making him sense something closing in on him. He couldn't see any tunnel, no trace of light touched him. Now he was the water itself. The milk carton being carried along in it. If he looked at the boat, then he was the boat. He was becoming the depths. The depths were dangerous, not only, but still, he was getting closer and closer to them. He was swimming along a seam that was getting ever darker. The seam teemed with faces and voices. He himself was this seam. He, Charles.

Brendan was doing his data checks. He had Charles, Mr Regular, firmly in his sights: 20:10 hours, Wind 220°, 16 knots, water temperature 17 degrees centigrade, air temperature 19 degrees, waves two feet high, pressure 1023 hPa, clouds to the left, clouds to the right, forecast: more wind, swell at least grade two. Meanwhile, their man was only managing seventy-five yards towards the coast every hour, everything else was just drift to the east. He, as pilot, looked ahead, looked after, posted, drew, steered, saved, suffered alongside, took joy in every single yard, like he always did, produced England's finest ginger biscuits, like he always did, and stayed awake night after night. He had the constitution of an ox, was unflappable in every sense. There was just one thing he hated about this job. The swimmer would get so far and with every entitlement think him or herself so close to the goal, and yet their swimming was all spent; it was all just current; and he had to take them out of the water. It broke his heart every time.

"We're steering southeast, but drifting north. We have to be honest," he said to Cedric when the lad joined him.

The second, lower curve of the S on the route had been looking too extended. For some time now.

"Tell it to him straight: we're not making any progress at all now?"

Side by side, they stared down into the water. They had done these trips together often enough to know that this journey too was now hanging in the balance: did the fish have the strength to swim into the morning?

Dumplings of darkness were growing between the waves. The blackness out of which these clumps had emerged was floating in the water as well as just above it. It flowed in twigs and veins, themselves formed when the darkness penetrated them. A foetal heart grew the same way, with the blood that nourished it also forging its own future pathways. From below, the veins spread upwards like saplings over the watery hillocks, lay themselves flat across the skins of the waves and, as each quivering ridge tipped, leaped vertically up and away. Ever more finely woven tissues of darkness lolled about on the Channel, like buoys. They washed around Charles' head on every breath.

Soon enough the inky water webs were rising into the air, flowing towards one another, merging. A seeping cloth, darkness was now also surging into the Channel from above. As if, having reflected the sky all day long, the sea was itself reflected in the giant arc of the atmosphere. The hour between eight and nine. The twilights of the sky and sea were bleeding into each other. Behind all this, the Channel wore an edging of silver and lead.

The spit in his mouth tasted of iron. The dark held no fear for him. Night swimming had been part of his training. He tried to steady himself with these phrases: Part of the training. No fear.

In his ears the waves were ringing, stronger on the left than on the right. The straining of the engine, pounding in his legs, had crowded out the rest of the outside world.

Brendan called, "9 p.m. feed!"

The world was filled with rays of inexpressible coolness and warmth.

Now he was pleasantly small. The neon light sticks were moving like a pair of wings a couple of inches below the sea's reflective surface. Charles was lying lower in the water than he had in all the hours previously. The Channel's floor was made of an eternal, melodic silence, a silence that hid so shyly and successfully beneath the beatings of the tides that hardly anyone even suspected its existence. The tiniest of sounds, the most careful of breaths was enough to break it, and yet there it was, even at shallow depths, present all of a sudden, undeniable, puzzling, a spreading cloud that emanated from far-flung, giant cauldrons of quiet which, should you look for them, you would never find.

What might Abbie look like today? Maude aged sixty-two was much more like her mother than Maude aged twenty. Perhaps the sisters too would have grown more alike? Maude, he considered, wasn't just pining for youth, wasn't just suffering the final throes of the menopause and its attendant vulnerabilities, or in the grip of a romantic dream. She wouldn't have needed Silas for any of that. Maude was pining for Abbie. She didn't want Charles to leave forever. He was supposed to know, accept, and stay. She had been aiming to start a different kind of family, a family of two-men-and-a-Maude. For a Maude that then could be both, Abbie and Maude.

This, he now realized, had been the offer right from the start. The thing he had run away from.

Charles the teaspoon.

What did Maude wish for, even though she might not fully grasp it, what did she see, without seeing through it, where was she climbing to in her dreams? The sea's cauldrons were echoing. He still figured in Maude's dreams, this he was sure of, climbed up and down ladders with her. "A bit crowded, our marriage," Diana, Princess of Wales, had said of her Charles and his Camilla, as she blinked with British understatement into the camera. Like the royals, they too had been a bit crowded right from the start. But in a wonderful variation: for them, three counted as downsizing.

Floating shards, spontaneous explosions, final sparks. The last hour of the evening turned out to be a kind of destruction that left everything intact. What a drama queen this hour was, particularly at sea. Not happy until the central star had set in one of those all-round, radiant displays that made it look like an orange-red spikey hedgehog. You couldn't help but want to lament the beauty of it all: Another day over! Charles was simply light-hearted. The eighteenth hour, and he was swimming. The longest attempted swim of his life. The most awful and the most lamentably beautiful. Donkey-fuzz-grey mats were besieging the horizon. The Channel reflected a rust-red on all its humps and lumps; darkness already reigned in the hollows between. You could not call them troughs, the water was swirling oily, flat.

Unperturbed, the *Henry*, eager, trusty pounding engine that it was, cast its lights straight ahead. Wherever the electric beam hit the water, depth was extinguished. Only the surface remained. The waves next to Charles, by contrast, were breathing. He counted his strokes, spoke to Maude. Orange stingrays of light were crossing the skies; arms of darkness encircled one another at sea, each searching the other out.

On the last feed he had replenished the Vaseline in his ears. It was like a plug. If Charles heard anything it was the wind, the water, the pulsing inside him, his own heart. The beating root that had started to pump when he was still a tadpole, no brain, no spine, just a pile of reproductive cells.

At the age of ten Charles had gone through a spell of setting his alarm for five in the morning. "The dead of night," the hour when even nocturnal hunters take a nap. As a student he had got up at this time to study. He called it "the hollow." Something came to rest, stretched out, softened. He was expecting this sensation to become more marked on water than on land as the night progressed. But unfortunately he no longer knew for sure what progress was.

Black water, hollows between the waves, thick and dark like oil. Yet overall the Channel refused to grow properly dark. The English and French coasts, so near, threw lights to one another over the wedge of water; the ships crossing in all directions lit up all directions; the sky shone a dirty yellow.

He swam.

And swam.

From feed to feed.

Midnight came.

He took ten seconds extra. Chocolate. Tea.

He swam.

At irregular intervals the whole surface of the sea rippled right across, as if fanned by a powerful bellows, the gentle sigh of a peaceful sleeper. Nothing as small as an animal or a human. The Channel itself was the putative sleeper, troubled by the horrendous traffic that barely ever abated, not even at night. Charles listened to it all, his arms now tracing the swimming motion as if it were the most natural thing in the world. Like breathing in your sleep.

Between the waves bobbed his eyes, his self.

Shouted loud and clear! Seventeen times, claimed the master of the journey. Only on the eleventh hour had he even reacted to his name.

Oh no!

He wasn't for fishing out. His only attempt.

He waved about.

"I'm fine," he declared. "Just look!"

Charles the Noodle, slightly stiffer than a few hours ago, but long, white, elegant. The water was carrying him, regardless whether it smelled of forest or kitchen or Maude. He elongated himself and swam. Something was swimming beside him.

Not flotsam, not a dolphin, not a whale, not a shark. He'd already been there. So it was nothing. Unimpressed by these sharp deductive skills, nothing swayed along beside him. He had felt its presence for a while but only realized now that he was feeling it. Did this sentence even make any sense? It was born of the water, that much was certain.

Whatever was slipping along beside him was still there.

It was accompanying him and it was quiet. He heard himself breathing and taking his strokes and felt the water swirling by him, and over it all he heard the *Henry*, travelling alongside. After so many hours, he hardly paid any attention to the noise of her engine anymore except that now, when he was trying to figure out what was taking a dip next to him, all he could hear was the boat and nothing but the boat.

Whatever was swimming next to him maintained an even distance, about ten feet he would have guessed, except how could anyone know what ten feet was after so many miles in the water and in any case it hardly mattered. He, Charles, was here, and *it* was here, swimming now to the left, now to the right of him.

How could that be?

He was afraid of the thing in the water, this I-beside-him or him-beside-me, this long, white figure, for that was how he imagined his counterpart, naked like him and tracking his course for quite some time.

But what could happen to him, it was almost like lying in bed down here, his legs just slightly bent, not like in the womb, not like a foetus, simply relaxed.

It could come to an end. It would come to an end. This swimming-alongside would be over too. And what did anyone think was going to happen?

He opened his eyes. There were three of these new escorts. A clutch of stars and a ridiculous half-moon, bathed in a calm, soulless light, hung over the scene.

The Channel reflected both the moonlight and the headlights of the *Henry*, and in this double light Charles saw that there really were three creatures circling him. They weren't long like him, but shorter and rounder; oval, to be precise. And yet, they weren't moving like fish, and so he had been right: not a fish, not a whale, not a jellyfish, not flotsam, not a roof ripped off someone's home.

"Look," he shouted up the ship's flank.

They would call him crazy. Shadows in the shadows of the water. He hadn't felt any approach. The three had simply been there, three feet below the surface, and he was awake like he hadn't been for hours, if awake meant sharing the same reality as the crew.

For at least the last few minutes, because he had been counting. Counting how many times they had circled round him. How many were there.

"Is he doubling up? Is he fading?" said his captain, standing next to Matilda at the railing. Stage two hypothermia? Or already stage three?

Hallucinations?

Cedric answered from the wheel-house. There was nothing on the radar, nothing at all, but he too had seen something.

"Three... three thingies!"

Tuna would have been the right size, almost the right shape too. But the *Henry* had been too close to the coast for too long for such fast swimmers, and the shadows were too solid. He sensed whatever was encircling him, pushing water aside, even though, however much he looked, he saw only darker darkness wherever it zoomed.

The circles were perfect. Whichever way he turned, his escorts maintained the same distance, both from one another and from him.

He used the next breath, the one to the left, given that now he was keeping to the right of the *Henry*, to shout one word up to the crew. The answer.

That would show them how alert he was. How far ahead of them.

He heard Brendan: "I don't believe it!"

And Matilda, answering: "You're right!"

Some of the warm blood that was still in circulation returned to his fingers. It was 01:30.

Then he had a drink. Matilda handled the surprise the best. She clipped back her yellow hair and said she was proud of him. That he was still so alert. And hadn't panicked, quite the opposite.

"Well done."

No one had said that to him for a very long time. He stretched and his fingertips were almost warm as they enclosed the pouch of drink.

Charley-Darley!

The pilot and log-lady leaned far out over the railing to him. Not even a mile to go to the French coast. The French were patrolling *La Manche* for illegal immigrants. For refugees.

Well that was a new one on him. Brendan sounded distracted.

Well swimming the Channel is a new one on me, thought Charles.

Matilda threw him an extra food pack down the line. Definitely: he liked teachers. This one here must have been excellent. Definitely: the darkness underwater was brighter than the darkness directly around his head. Bright the boat, its shadow deepest black. Next to Charles, purple feathered seagrass waved in the wind, spikey, broken, beautiful. He rolled under the dark sky studded with holes for stars, rolled over it. He was feeling at ease.

The pilot's eyes followed the grotesquely pink pouch that was swinging its way over to Charles by the light of Matilda's torch. The rest of what he saw was disgusting, but at least perfectly so: an exhausted swimmer surrounded by three drones. A lousy scene, excellent composition. How skilfully the machines copied the man's every move. Programmed on people. As if the Channel weren't already an overdetermined force stacked against every human being, even without the aid of intelligent metal spyware. He felt like he had suddenly seen a truth for all mankind. Everyone had shadows flying around their heads, their bodies. Accompanying them every step of the way. All their lives long.

Charles sucked deliberately slowly on the packet, he didn't just want to ingest the food, he wanted the picture too: the boat, the hunters, himself. Their quarry brought to bay. What a blessing! Now he didn't need to sweettalk his pilot, beg for one last chance. He had proven that he was still the full shilling. He, of all of them, the madman in the salty broth, in the dark, in his dream, was ahead of the game.

The reflection from the light sticks glistened along the water's skin. Yet another plane queuing for London split the sky over his head in two. In between Charles' breaths only the most agreeable of voices and spectres now had their place. His father arrived home for Christmas with an enormous lobster, which sadly also meant it was very old. Usually carp were for the pot on Christmas Day, because the family needed scales, lots of scales, to wrangle enough good luck into the kitty to last the year. A Polish custom. Grandpa preferred lobster, it reminded him of the sea and he ate more of the tough beast than anyone else at the table. Blind, the brown shell-boat of a creature had moved its asymmetrical claws in the bathtub as helplessly as a refugee. If any of the claws fell off, the Crustacean would grow another to take its place. Humans had yet to manage this. "Smart arrangement," said Grandpa, "also, the males are substantially fatter than the females." "The lucky creatures come with a carapace," said Charles' father. His mother replied, "but they shed it." And so each could be right on their own terms. Grandpa had swum the Dnieper to escape Stalin, had sat things out in the mountains of French-Switzerland, lived in Brussels, in Geneva, all the cities that were witness to the birth of modern Europe. Charles, the youngest in the clan, raised in England in a polyglot English-Austrian family had, hardly unexpectedly, barely finished his studies before he moved to Germany with his northern English, one-quarter Scottish, Viennese-educated wife. Here, he worked at the University of Düsseldorf for over twenty years until, to his own surprise, he returned to the English-Scottish-Welsh island.

If you lived on an island, said Grandpa, you would be well advised to be able to swim to the next shore. Even before his grandson could walk properly he took him to the sea; he registered the five year-old for Camden swimming club. The teacher got his new pupils to line up in order of size then had each end of the line pair up, one from the left, one from the right. The unequal pair, one tall, one short, was assigned a changing locker: not only did they have to share a key but also their swimming careers; they were to encourage, spur on and protect one another. The blond-haired boy who was paired with Charles, a head taller and a year older, said, "What are you doing here, tadpole?"

"Beating you!"

And that was how they had met, he and Silas.

She had been surprised but let him in when he told her he was heading off on a journey that might take some time and wanted to talk to her. Once more they had sat in the kitchen, Maude had switched on the light in the cooker hood, casting the table more deeply into green shadow. Early August, early in the evening. Rain clouds were gathering over the slope.

"When I read your letter? Back then, in Vienna?"

She rubbed the back of her neck. He hadn't seen this gesture for a long time. Maude had been teaching too much. She was tired.

She had sensed something of him in it. Something like … uncertainty. She had seen how he shook, she said, with feelings for her. This had both flattered and unnerved her. And so she had become curious. Had he been expecting something more in her reply? Well, she was sorry, but she didn't have anything more to offer: excited anticipation.

"You were the tough one. You, not Silas."

She had been reminded of what she had seen when she first set eyes on him. How he had lain on his towel at the side of the Westerland pool, Silas' shadow on his sleeping body. His best friend, Silas had said, amazing Chemist, totally reliable, he loved him, the old frog-face.

Maude's eyes had taken on a different kind of expression. Violet and grey tones shimmered in her iris, yielding a deeper, though more fickle sheen.

And so after she and Silas had parted, sadly but on friendly terms, she had travelled on to Oxford. And that's where the crows had torn open their beaks. And then Charles had appeared at the side of the road as she was leaving and she had seen the love in his face, helpless and huge. And everything had tipped.

This, she said, had started happening to her with some regularity since Abbie's death. Wham, regardless of where she was, what she was thinking or doing, a cosmic vacuum cleaner of misery would appear and suck all colour and movement from her surroundings. Only a reality in slow motion remained, sad, senseless, heavy.

Tipped on the bus as she left Oxford. Tipped, even if only for the vacuum cleaner to show her what it might yet do. Instead of drifting for hours, as if submerged behind glass because she, Maude, no longer belonged in this world, she got off the bus at the airport and found a world that was once more filled with voices and sparkle; alive. Almost like before Abbie's accident. But only almost. And this, she said, had been … progress. Alive, without shutting out her sister's death or denying it. In this moment of return and unexpectedly widened perspective she had seen Charles' face, the way he had stood on the pavement to wave to her one last time, and she had felt his closeness.

For more than a year she had lived with reality constantly tipping. The second tipping, the one associated with him, had always helped counter the first. Even if he didn't know … it was in spite of everything …

"Well," she said, "you never let me down."

No, Silas was not in the house. They weren't living together, not the way Charles probably imagined it. Silas was living in France, she said, on airplanes, travelling and sometimes in London. Yes, then he did sleep in her bed. The new bed in her room.

"Before you start thinking it's this way or that, it's better for you to know how things really are."

It had felt awkward with Silas, she said, when he reappeared in Düsseldorf. A Silas-ghost who frightened her because he reminded her of Abbie, the time they had spent together as a foursome. But for exactly the same reason she had also found herself drawn to her former friend and lover. Gradually she had rediscovered what she had always liked about Silas. She was pleased to find something old in her that, to her surprise, obviously still lived on. It had been a wonderful revelation, she said: how the twenty-year-old Maude still had a voice, a set of senses and emotions inside her, the woman who was then in her fifties. And Abbie too. Whom she had missed more sorely than she had wanted to admit. With Silas Abbie had returned. Perhaps precisely because the two of them, as far as Silas and Abbie and Tex were concerned, had decidedly mixed feelings. Right? They had never discussed it but nevertheless she was certain, no, she knew, that this was something they shared.

"We," said Maude, "were us, Maude and Charles, all the time there was just the two of us." In the living room, however, with Silas, there had been more than three. It had felt, Maude said, as if Abbie were part of the circle, "as if she were living on through the three of us."

It had been a bodily sensation. And he knew, didn't he, that she didn't believe in ghosts.

He would have liked to look her in the eye. But she had bowed her head. The state of indecision that had been tormenting him and distorting their relationship for the last few months lifted slightly.

"There was a *Tante-Emma-Laden* near where our parents lived in Newcastle." Maude used the German word for corner shop. "The woman running the shop was the butt of everyone's jokes. She had two men, both her age. And both ugly! The men were an even greater source of ridicule than she was. The three of them would not be swayed. The village imagined everything, down to the last detail. Everything. For maybe half a year. Then it was forgotten."

She had bowed her head even more, rolled it gently from side to side. Speaking into her chest she said, "Why couldn't we do that too?" And added, as if it were the most natural thing in the world, "Abbie would agree. If she were in my shoes, that's exactly what she would have done."

He was so stunned by this association that he stupidly asked, "Where?"

Clearly, Maude had changed.

"Here," she said. "We could all do with a home."

2:13 a.m. The current vanished. Brendan called out that he had noticed the *Henry* yawing; meanwhile the instruments had picked it up too.

"You've nothing pulling at you anymore!"

He was sixty-two years old and drifting on the sea, in August, in the middle of the night. It was the longest night of his life and he was testing just how much further he could stretch. All his tendons hurt; he could no longer detect his muscles. Hadn't Abigail's story brought it home to him (not taught, but brought home, impressed upon him) that the path through life, if there were such a thing, always went through your body and that ultimately no-one knew what a body was, what it meant?

Matilda counted, at Brendan's request, Charles' stroke rate, while the pilot once more compared his data with the map. It was half past two. There was no way they would make Gris-Nez, with a bit of luck it would be Wissant. It mustn't be Calais, the morning traffic was too heavy and there was no landing place for the *Henry* with its fragile outrigger, made of man. The captain's thoughts clinked like coins in a machine. It was routine, always the same factors to weigh up, but with a different factor at the centre each time, a different body, a different story before, after and during the swim, and he, Brendan, constantly had to reconsider what to say, "keep going" or "game over."

It could tip from one moment to the next.

Charles saw his pilot stepping up to the railing. He would notice straight away that he wasn't swimming properly anymore. He had his excuse at the ready: can't anyone take a leak around here…

The man simply said, "We'll wait for the tide to carry you and the *Henry* towards land. You need the current. It's your last chance."

Charles rejoiced. Inwardly. He no longer had the energy for outward signs of celebration. That was nice. His inner self was now clearly defined. Well, that was an additional finding. It had been a thing of total indifference to him for the majority of his life. And it was also really nice that he no longer needed to advance in the world above. Just keep his head periodically above water long enough to breathe. One and a half hours to go.

If it continued like this.

"It" was him.

"Charley," said Maude, "it's your move."

"You're very tired."

Cedric at the railing. The railing directly above Charles.

"You're not ev… lifting your arm above the water."

"I don't understand."

"We're showing you where to go but you're not swimming." Brendan.

Charles raised his arm to wave to him.

The silhouetted heads above him were calling him, he couldn't distinguish who was saying what, which voice was who.

He was getting colder. Then he remembered: he must keep moving. The tide, the moon, your mind. Perhaps he should run through his multiplication tables, all the way up, all the way down, 9 x 9, 8 x 9, 7 x 9 … Say right now where to find the dodo foot in the Natural History Museum. Come up, right away, with the name of the third whale that hangs from the ceiling there. The whales in the museum had been alive, even though they were only skeletons. Exposed thoraxes, curved ribs, holes and nothing, and yet they were floating up there, flying through the air. He swam as if he were one of those maritime spirits, a skeletal structure filled with residual thoughts, oxygen and emotions, carefully moving its jaw and tearing music from its bones. His will was slow, but it was there. The tip of his penis reached far into his chest, while his nerves, after so many hours in the water, after this battle, this metamorphosis into crust, movement and salt, were growing out incrementally from his body, as if they wanted to float around him like a coat of finest cloth, of coral almost. This exodus appalled and pleased him in equal measure; another source of wonder.

"You're treading water."

"You won't get anywhere like that. The tide alone won't wash you up on the beach."

"… the honest truth."

"That's…"

"… 2:55 a.m."

"Come in!"

"Up here."

He flinched: Brendan. Brendan next to him. How could that be? Was the pilot sitting in the dinghy?

"Come. Come in!"

Coo, coo, Charley!

But Charles was no pigeon. He perceived everything with searing clarity. He knew their thoughts before they had even had them. Ahead of him, the French coast shone, while along the horizon to the left dawn was breaking. Remnants of the grease clung to his body. The beauty of his solitude too.

"Out!"

To the right, darkness reigned. To the right was coast.

"I mean it!"

They must have got muddled up. Feed time wasn't for another five minutes.

He dived down, to the left. 2:55 a.m. sounded wonderful. Coast sounded wonderful. He repeated it to himself. Within touching distance. Perhaps a little too dark to see it. As if by way of compensation, he could feel the coast. The bottom of the sea was rising. Although still a considerable depth below him. Thirty feet? Twelve? He could feel it, no question. Calais, where else. Bays and sand. So much better than the grey nose that consisted of nothing but steep cliffs.

"Listen to me."

But of course, Freda! Crawl onto land. Polish your balls! A promise is a promise. And what a promise! He would tell her about it when he saw her again. It would be light then.

"Hell."

"Out!"

He dived down. Hadn't he just done that? Someone laughed. He heard somebody laughing. A woman's voice. She said that it

was 7:00 a.m.

"Breakfast!"

"Hmm," he said.

Just in case she decided to ask him again how he was feeling.

She kept asking that. He had hardly woken up before she asked. He had sent her away. Now she was back again.

It was light.

Breakfast was served in his B&B from eight o'clock onwards. He would get a double serving, that's what his hosts had promised him. To make up for yesterday's missed breakfast. To celebrate his crossing.

That had been a crushing defeat.

Now he knew where that expression came from. His heart was being crushed.

His hosts would pretend not to know anything. But they were just as much in the know as anybody else who had the ship's name. Tracking, global positioning, that social shit.

"Yeah, that's right. Total exhaustion. Like a dead fish in the water. They pulled me out fifty yards from the coast. Try again next year? Thanks."

And with that he would stop them going down the path of consolation.

They would reply that they were celebrating his safe return to the breakfast parlour. Well he didn't doubt that. They made their living out of people like him.

He slid over to the railing and leaned against the cool metal. It was obviously enough for Matilda to see him leaving the horizontal for her English morning reflexes to be triggered – she shoved a thermos cup in his hand. Steaming tea. Even through the sunglasses on his nose (and where had they come from?) the cliffs looked overly white. The *Henry* was heading directly for them. The Channel was playing at being a sheep, curly licks instead of waves.

"Pros," said Matilda. She had probably said more before this. If he kept his mouth shut now, perhaps she would repeat it. That would help him cover up that he had no idea how he had ended up here. Pros! He would thank Cedric and Brendan, he too was a pro. Now he was shaking again. Like a pro, he clung on to the cup, let his teeth chatter against the thermal rim. He couldn't stop it. He pushed his tongue into the chattering, smiled at Matilda, waited for more. His tongue was twice as large as normal.

The teacher grinned at him. The sunglasses suited him, she said. He went to raise his arm automatically, stopped halfway. So they were hers? Those pink ones? Charles, totally destroyed, a crushing defeat, sat, too weak to do so without support, at the railing of the *Henry* wearing a pair of pink sunglasses and being ferried back to Dover. What a hero. He tried to say something. He might have succeeded, had he managed to part his lips just a little more. But some sound at least came from the back of his throat. A seagull spurted away, flying low over the water.

6:13 a.m.

"Charles, Charley, come on!"

"It's light."

"Open your eyes, mate."

A woman's voice. That's right, said part of his head. There had been a teacher on board.

Not such an easy ask, the eyes. The lids were stuck. Someone (Cedric?) shoved a pair of glasses onto his nose.

Bright: to the right of him, to the left of him. He slumped back down. Bright above him, ahead of him.

He felt himself lying. Opposite him, a towel was hanging on the railing, sky blue. He blinked. A pink green morning on the horizon.

Hadn't someone just been talking about stormy weather?

Not even the cliffs were wobbling.

The cliffs?

Cliffs in front of him. The white braid on England's warring shoulder; the row of teeth bared; sea creatures, thousands of years old, stacked up on top of each other. The hard part.

The dramatic beginning. The end. It was already white. The sun was shining.

His end.

How late?

Something had croaked out this question.

"Ah," said the woman's voice, "here we are."

A quarter past six. Yellow and pink, right next to his head. He was starting to see more clearly now.

6:00 a.m.

She had covered him up, stuffed the ends of the blanket under his body so that it was held in place by his bodyweight, and checked on him every fifteen minutes. No movement for the last hour, not even a flicker from his eyelids. So this was what it looked like when a dream was shattered. She knew how it felt but had never observed it so closely in somebody else. The night for her had had a singular focus, centred exclusively on itself. Someone had to get into the water, not her; somebody had to steer, not her; somebody had to save the boat, not her. The waves didn't allow for more than bobbing up and down. Another one and a half hours and then they would be back in the grip of Dover's beach music, Dover's cream gulls, Dover's petty trading frenzy. The *Henry*'s route resembled a finger. The finger had almost touched France, missed it by an inch, tracing one route over, abandoned just before the finish, and then another route back, parallel to the first. The engine phut-phutted along like a trusty donkey, the clouds flew ahead of them towards England. The sea lay there, as if it too were taking a rest.

5:25 a.m.

Something the colour of gneiss ballooned out, dark and shadowy. It swung, moved away, turned back, was coming straight for him. He too was lying. Something was hard. He was lying down, it was windy. He was lying in a bed. Through the window to his left light fell. He had just moved

175

back in to Number 8. Narrow, the bed. Silas had to travel with his tea trade. And then Maude was off, to another concert, and Charles would spend a few days alone with Silas in the house. He had told them about his swim. The blue planet: water, water, hardly any land. Meaning: cliffs, continental shelf, firmness, constantly licked by H_2O. Dykes all the rage, he had said, fear of flooding. Humankind was sitting once more in Noah's ark, now grudgingly acknowledged. Some people had fearfully returned to feeding pigeons. Others were grilling meat.

His words sounded like he was drunk.

Straight away he conceded: some people fired up barbecues because it was tasty. At least, Silas and he found it tasty. After he had made landfall on Mount Ararat, Noah had begun by sticking some of the superfluous sheep and goats on the spit. For Yahweh.

"Loaded his ark with foresight," said Silas. The business man through and through.

The term "business man" referred to Noah and to God. Who had given the captain of the ark the most exact of instructions. "Salvation included. The old fox."

"Ah, fox," said Maude.

Charles looked at her. He was thinking something, but wasn't sure what. Fox? Something brushed past him. Momentarily his bed felt as if it were made of deck planks.

Were they both turning religious on her now, asked Maude.

"Soul," said Charles. Free soul. A pivotal concept. Also called adventurous soul. They, the men, had one and were planning a barbecue.

"God likes meat," said Silas. At least, Noah's God did. The God of business deals.

"Yahweh was no vegetarian," Charles added.

And that, said Maude, was the grand revelation from all his Channel swimming madness?

Silas laughed. Their conversations had changed. But not fundamentally. Their jokes flowed less easily now.

Silas said that he, Silas, was the opposite of vegetarian. And, therefore, not the opposite of God. This realisation pleased him.

Maude said soon Silas would be as cracked as Charles.

Charles said he was endeavouring to keep his lead.

Nobody any longer pretended things were as before. One weight rose, another dropped. They had got the hang of this now. It was equally clear that every movement left a trace. A second chin? A spreading middle? Sampo the Setter was older than them but had never had to concern himself with this stuff about the weights. He rejoiced. Which took the form of a small puddle on the floor. How else should a dog rejoice? In any case, the animal really was old. And deeper down, deeper into the any case that only applies to animals anyway, the dog was boundlessly happy: everyone was home.

Family number two: less order, more merriment. Charles also found himself more and more often idiotically content.

Idiot. That had been the answer.

5:05 a.m.

How quiet it was. He sensed the vibrations of the boat's engine, but he couldn't hear it. Cedric was steering, everyone else was asleep. When he had wanted to sleep, they hadn't

177

allowed him. Now that he could, he lay awake. Wide awake. Wired. He could sense the deck planks on some parts of his body and not on others. The backs of his thighs were numb, his back was numb. The back of his head wasn't. Some parts of him were floating. But at least he was out in the fresh air. He had made them tie him to the railing by a rope slung around his ankle. If he looked to the side, he could see the Channel. It didn't matter which side. Inwardly he was still swaying. Ahead of him, the first rays of the morning sun were sharpening the damn cliffs: ever steeper, an ever brighter white. He tore his eyes shut.

5:00 a.m.

His lips pressed together (= he felt from the inside), his face narrower, thinner, hollower than at the start (= he felt from the inside), stretched out on the deck (= he felt from the inside), small (= he felt everywhere). His entire body had shrunk. Charles, lying, as the essence-of-Charles: a light blue blanket, a red beanie, white stubble. He could see it from the outside. Charles the Camera floated above things, Charles the Swimmer swam through them, Charles the Failure, finally released from the wheelhouse, wanted to curl up into a ball but was too stiff for that. They had placed his phone next to him, his wallet, his watch, his ID, his cap and the pair of light sticks. As if he were dead. He was dead, he was lying down. Something was swaying. Was he swaying? He felt for the sticks. Feeling his way worked, not seeing. He thrust them out to sea. That was a thought. Nothing happened. If something had happened, he would have heard it. Too bad,

Charles! Charles the Dregs, Charles the Failure couldn't even raise his arm.

4:50 a.m.

Matilda said it didn't make sense for her to keep going back and forth between the cabin and his spot. The journey back to England, into the morning, was very pleasant, she would be happy to stay out with him. She was awake in any case. Wide awake. The journey had been very refreshing. Flushed her system right through! It would take them three hours to get back home, just he wait. That's how far he had come.

He swallowed. In as much as this was possible. She was trying to comfort him and was making things worse. It didn't matter. Everything hurt anyway.

She had tied the pink cloth around her head, was sitting on a small stool next to him and entering data into her columns.

Nonsense, she said, it was August, 4:50 a.m., didn't he see the dawn?

"Come on then," she said.

She sat there, sibylline.

She didn't intend for one moment that he should do anything, anything as real as stretching out his arm and holding still. Rather, she reached for his hand, turned it around and placed a finger on his pulse. Silently she moved her lips. They hadn't liked his breathing. They had forced him to stay sitting in the cabin and drink.

Ginger tea, ginger biscuits, a sick bag.

The cliffs pushed themselves as shadows against the sky. He wasn't swimming in a circle. He wasn't swimming at all. He wanted to be alone.

"All the same," she said, "one more swim!" One last time, today. Back onto land at Samphire Hoe. They would row him over, if he preferred.

His pulse had been measured. Charley-Darley, half-alive, at 53! From now on she would only check every half hour.

"Do you know Freda?" he asked.

And immediately thought, what rubbish, Matilda only moved to Dover a few weeks ago.

"Of course," she said. She had heard a lot about her. And heard her a lot. At the marina, where else?

Charles was as sick and as happy as a dog. The swaying was coming from everywhere. He mustn't stare into the face in front of him, that made it all worse.

"Don't you sleep?"

"I'm a bird, I sleep with my eyes open."

Now that she said it, he could see it. Matilda was a bird. Maude a fox. Matilda, who sat up in one fluid, effortless movement, smiled at him. The dinghy behind her, to the right, swayed on its frame.

It was just a dinghy.

4:30 a.m.

The sound brought him back.

The sound of water.

As if he hadn't heard enough of that.

It was raining. The rain was landing on wood. Next to him. So he must be lying on wood. And in the rain. Which would mean he was no longer swimming. He was no longer in the water.

Water was falling on him. Water with holes. H_2O, N_2, He, Ar, CO_2.

Even as a child he had liked nothing better than to lie in bed and listen to the rain beating against the window pane. Against the branches in front of the pane and against the glass, and therefore also a little against himself, against his self and his thoughts. And the way the words and the self in these thoughts paraded around like figurines. He was lying on wood and rain was falling on it. The wood formed the deck of the *Henry*. He was lying on the deck of the *Henry*, and it was dark and raining, and he was swimming in the rain.

Which he didn't feel. He was so soaked through that he no longer felt any moisture. He wasn't swimming, he was lying still. The rain was coming down on him and down next to him, and nothing was on the slide. He heard the rain.

He breathed in. He breathed out.

3:55 a.m.
He had swum forever. He remembered it all. The last mile, the light. He had sensed the land coming closer. The Channel changed, the coast reached out. He remembered. He could sense things that lay both in him and beyond him.

3:50 a.m.
Breakers sprayed over the railing, they were travelling in a loop to show him the grey horn, the nose, that he had missed, so that he would believe them = he didn't make it. Rough sea, waves almost six feet high, couldn't he tell?

The pilot was sitting next to him. Cedric blocked the cabin door.

They said he was alright. That's what they said.

But he mustn't sleep. He was wedged into the chair. To the right the cabin wall, behind him the chair's back, to the left his life-man. If he slumped forward, they propped him back up and poured something hot into him. Everything was hot. The air that he was breathing burned. He couldn't speak. Or didn't want to.

3:45 a.m.

He fell down a stairs with Hazel in his arms, yanked the child up high, they lay at the bottom, the baby cried, didn't suffer even a scratch. He had plenty of scratches and bruises, he hadn't broken his fall, just saved his daughter, he wasn't a completely bad person.

Brendan stood next to him, something yellowy-pink hovered in the doorway. They were in the cabin, manoeuvring him onto a chair. Cedric must be holding the wheel.

Brendan said, "Charley, give us a story. Just another word!"

Had he, Charles, said anything? He didn't think so.

"Sure," said Matilda, "a ladder and rocks. So beautiful."

3:38 a.m.

"We're losing him."

"Get that chair! There, now he can't fall."

"Keep him awake!"

"He has to talk. Ask him something."

"Doesn't he have a family?"

"Ask him about his child."

"She's already grown up."

"Ask him about his fucking child!"

3:20 a.m.

It had been raining for hours. Hazel was sitting in her tent in the giant serving bowl, waiting for the sea. He slipped into the bowl beside her. His daughter was looking at a photo. Hesitantly she passed it over to him, reverse-side up, when he asked. Maude's handwriting, in pencil: Rantum 1976. The picture showed all four of them, arm in arm. He and Silas in the middle, Abigail on one side, Maude on the other.

He with Maude, Silas with Abigail.

Hazel had rummaged in the forbidden chest at home to find the picture. He didn't tell her off. Who is the woman, she wanted to know.

"She looks like me."

He disagreed.

"But you look really in love with her."

That was the first time he had heard this phrase from Hazel's mouth.

"Do you know what that means, to be in love?," he asked.

She shook her head.

"Me neither," he said.

3:18 a.m.

"When's your birthday?"

"What's the name of your dog?"

He hoped Cedric hadn't noticed. His face was so swollen, no one could notice a thing.

They knew in any case that he couldn't speak.

He was crying.

3:15 a.m.

He was wearing trousers. They smelled familiar. His trousers. He had brought them with him. He was shivering in his trousers. In his jacket. Brought that along too. The blanket around his shoulders belonged to the ship. Brendan was steering. The first hour after the retrieval had to be spent sitting upright. Retrieval: the word was ricocheting around his head like a squash ball gone rogue on court. Retrieval! As if he had been found again. His head was misty and shining. He was a bowl, just as the fog had been. Only firmer. Hopefully firmer. He could see the bowl from inside, was sitting in its midst.

Retrieval bounced around the white inside of his skull, going round and round in circles.

"Rescued," his pilot said.

The old pair of trousers pinched at the waist. The blanket smelled of salt. "He's waking up," said a woman's voice next to him. He hadn't noticed that there was a third person.

"Bring some old things with you for the return journey, things that can get covered in Vaseline. You'll throw them away afterwards."

Old things that smelled of Maude's detergent. It had been a mistake to bring these old things along.

Was he crying? He wasn't sure. It felt like crying, in his eyes. But not underneath his eyes. He was so moist that he couldn't sense any more moisture.

3:13 a.m.

Hands were holding him, pulling off his trunks, rubbing him down. "I've seen a few naked men in my life, you know, my dear!" Something turned him round, trousers, socks, where did those come from, with his left ear he heard "sit down," he was to sit upright, "stay, drink!," he didn't want any tea, "take it," he wanted to sleep, a belly was pressed against his head, or did his head fall against the belly, he opened his mouth, his mouth was already open, he said something, he couldn't hear anything, he couldn't see anything, he hadn't made it.

3:11 a.m.

Slowly he managed to open his eyes. His goggles were gone. He passed his hand over his face. His face was gone. His hand passed. His hand was gone. He felt nothing.

Faces swum around him, painted with shadows, as if wearing some kind of complicated visor.

3:08 a.m.

"It's alright."

"You're on the boat, Charles. He keeps kicking."

"He's cramping."

"Charles! Stop swimming."

"Stop!"

"DO YOU HEAR ME?"

3:06 a.m.

He was climbing down a ladder, the ladder had hands, he fell against a wall, something shook him, held his legs, straight-

ened them, he had to … "hold him" … "hell, he's kicking" …
he relented, but only out of weakness, he let himself fall,
over, done, let, let

3:05 a.m.
"He's gone."
   "But he's breathing."
   "Slap him in the face."

3:03 a.m.
"How long?," asked Matilda.
   "Two minutes."
   She didn't understand. Didn't people who were drowning
automatically rise back to the surface? Three times?
   "Sweetie," panted Brendan, "why do you think we have
him?"

3:02 a.m.
He was shrinking. A bird was sitting on a branch passing by
overhead. One hand after the other, "till you grab the sand."
When he reached the branch, the bird was a cloud. He
grabbed it.

3:01 a.m.
"Hold tight!"
   "Can you see him?"
   …
   …
   "Got him?"
   "No … fuck!"

2:58 a.m.

"He's, blimey … Brenny … he's gone!"

2:55 a.m.

"Come in!"

  "Up here."

2:56 a.m.

A pale reflection broke the perfection of darkness. Sampo, his head on Charles' lap, looking lovingly at him. It made Charles happy to realize that time had now become so limp and soft that it was touching itself.

2:57 a.m.

The reflection turned into a floating line, similar to the stripe on a deep-sea fish that had lost its way. Soon a second line, of similar, equally increasing length, appeared beneath it, slightly to the side; between the two stretched vertical rungs. It was clearly recognisable now: a ladder.

2:59 a.m.

Something was swimming beside him. Not a fish not a whale not a shark not a jellyfish not flotsam not a corrugated iron roof not a drone. Nothing that would try to grab him. It also wasn't him. Not himself, not his body. He was not afraid any more.

He was like Jim Button and the far-away giant. The giant had been a giant from afar. But the nearer you got to him, the smaller he became. Something was circling around him, accompanying him, pulling him. If he opened his eyes he couldn't see it. So he kept them closed. It was pointing him in a direction that he saw without his eyes.

He called this direction "ladder."

2:59 a.m.

It didn't reach up to the sky, but down, into the depths of the sea. A pretty ladder. He climbed, held tight, climbed. It got easier and easier.

2:59 a.m.

He was swimming. He was the water line in the glass between half full and half empty. Something lay ahead or behind. He had run out of energy to think about it now, nor did he have to.

3:01 a.m.

He was swimming.

3:01 a.m.

He was swimming. He was shrinking.

Freda was there. She waved at him. Her lips shone as pink as if they were about to burst into song at any moment. At any moment.

He climbed along the ladder.

3:01 a.m.

He was swimming. He was now

3:01 a.m.

very small

3:01 a.m.

very

over

and

ou

t

t

t

t

t

Tide. Speed. Position.

Position, state of the moon, prognosis. Something cold was returning in waves. He gathered all the dryness within him to point in one direction.

Balls over the sand, he wasn't letting this one go. Crawl on his bones, whistle out of his last orifice, bring on the grim pleasure. He would have whistled for joy, had he still been able to pucker his lips.

Brendan was there. Of course. Behind him, on the boat. "Look. See." It was just a few yards now.

The Channel shone like a Damascus blade and the waves ran as eagerly towards the shore as if they had an actual finish line rather than mere directional flow. The red of the morning sky touched water, rocks, bushes; unlike the daylight, it broke where it landed. It didn't care; it was young and readily forgot itself.

The water frothing back at him from the first rocky outcrops was a brownish green. Land too had its undercurrents, strata of oxides and mud.

Colourful, poisonous berries and rusty brown tangles of autumn lay between the rocks, as if the French summer were shorter than the English one. He discovered similar spots of colour on his arm. Warm, welcome, mucky mess. Troughs, terraces, steps leading to ledges of the most perfect, driest of greens – every hollow struck him as enormous. He dragged himself onto land like a lizard and let the sun warm his thick, scaly back until his stubby limbs were twitching again with energy.

For a few seconds he couldn't distinguish whether or not he was wearing a wetsuit. His heart raced. He was wearing one, even though it was forbidden.

This was nonsense, of course. It was because he was standing up and light was falling directly onto his skin again.

Clumsy, stiff.

Like a stork in a salad he stalked from stone to stone.

A world made of nothing but air, colour, light. Upright? He was swaying more than he was walking, he dropped down onto all fours. Safer that way. You crawled onto land.

A bird – a sandpiper? A plover? – was pecking about almost within touching distance. At sea all birds were white, as if more effort were pointless at this density of rays; over land they regained their colour. He wasn't sure if this was the product of the landscape, the sky, or his ocular faculties. To his right and his left, bands of blue-tinged shadows cast miniature woods and charming hollows all along the motionless hills.

His bones were thawing. A fluorescent cloud appeared, was mirrored in a rock pool, flew away backwards. Balls over French sand!

Every pebble knocked his feet into a stumbling rhythm, caught between the water and the land; the few trees in the distance bobbed about, like staggering pieces of chalk.

The ground was too firm for a body that had been swaying to and fro for more than twenty-four hours.

The sun was so high that the water had begun to glisten. The blue of the sky waited behind a shimmering, billowing white the colour of tin. Rocks bathed in raspberry light blocked his path, some came up to his waist, others only halfway up his shin. The sea had become a bedazzling mass of chlorophyll, stuffed with succulent bushy growths on hard ground. Sunshine cut through the wedges from below, like a knife through sheet metal.

His ring finger was bleeding, his right foot, this weakling, was stinging.

A miracle: he noticed.

The *Henry* was anchored behind him. When it sounded its horn he had to paddle back, forty yards maybe, grab the ladder, climb up. Brendan, luminous yellow t-shirt, large brown sunglasses, would lean on the railing and watch him.

Beyond the first stones that stood to attention like a group of meerkats there opened up a flatter, grey expanse of pebbles and erratic boulders. He reached a rock offering a hollow seat at the ideal height. He had twenty minutes grace, here everyone was covered by the law of shipwrecks. His head stuttered, lolled on his neck vertebrae, a Lego head. He removed his cap.

The land was supernaturally quiet.

He threw a pebble into the air, towards the water, it barely flew any distance, he had no strength left in his arm. But he had an arm. In the air.

His knees were like Christmas pudding: soft where they were supposed to be firm. In the parts that were supposed to be soft: grit and grease. Twenty minutes on a rock. Charles the Seal.

Grandpa had been a big fan of Odysseus. The sea. See!

As an old man, Odysseus had sat on the beach at Ithaca. Arrived back home, his head was still full of journeys. Nothing in the house was as he had left it, only the dog cared to recognize him, the maid. His father's jars of honey and home-brewed berry schnaps had still stood golden-yellow in the kitchen when Odysseus had had himself immured in the palace's cellar. It had been a bid to evade Menelaus' pursuers, his own cunning, himself. It had failed, and the madman who ploughed his field with constant about-turns and standing in for his ox, the madman who hummed away for days at a time at the bottom of the lime pit, had had to concede defeat. Now the battles, the journeys, and the saltwater were all beating on his bones as if they were playing the xylophone.

He scooped up some of the water into his hands as it trickled through the rockface.

The sun shone, midges swarmed around him. What an incredibly sweet sound.

This was the hum of the land. The earth. In twenty minutes he had to move on.

The rushing in his ear: abated.

Maude: abated.

Silas, Charles: everything abated.

The sea transformed itself into a vast and impenetrable piece of machinery, a fluid mechanism glistening in all its moving parts. The periodic explosions of morning light revealed it for what it was: the planet's gear box, connecting and transmitting the sun's energy.

Spots of happiness swapped places with zones of spite .

Gulls blitzed down upon the tide, drank, wheeled away again. Under their cries, the Channel buckled into a monumental lens encasing everything in a glass the purest of blue. The water's liquid power surged, and yet the English Channel was not the source of this vigour. Rather, unpredictability flowed through it, loosed from the depths, as a current of its own making.

All these beauties, the transience and the bewilderment they entailed, leapt at him and coursed through him and carried him away.

About the Author and Translator

One of Germany's most acclaimed poets and novelists, ULRIKE DRAESNER has been awarded the Nicolas Born Prize (2016), the Gertrud Kolmar Prize for Poetry (2019), the Bavarian Book Prize (2020), the Grand Prize of the German Literature Fund (2021), and the Literature Prize of the Konrad-Adenauer-Foundation (2024), among others. Her many novels and poetry collections include: *zu lieben* (2024), *Die Verwandelten* (2023), *hell & hörig* (2022), *Schwitters* (2020), and *subsong* (2014). A member of the German Academy for Language and Poetry, she has been a poet in residence at Goethe University Frankfurt, the University of Oxford, Dartmouth College, and the University of Wisconsin-Madison. She is a professor of creative writing at Deutsches Literaturinstitut Leipzig and resides in Berlin.

REBECCA BRAUN is Established Professor of German and World Literature at the University of Galway, Ireland. An expert on the production and reception of literature, she has worked extensively with contemporary writers, translators and individuals across the publishing chain. Her many publications include *World Authorship* (2020) and *Authors and the World: Literary Authorship in Modern Germany* (2022). This is her third book-length translation.

Also Available from UWSP

- *November Rose: A Speech on Death by Kathrin Stengel* (2008 Independent Publisher Book Award)
- *November-Rose: Eine Rede über den Tod* by Kathrin Stengel
- *Philosophical Fragments of a Contemporary Life* by Julien David
- *17 Vorurteile, die wir Deutschen gegen Amerika und die Amerikaner haben und die so nicht ganz stimmen können* by Misha Waiman
- *The DNA of Prejudice: On the One and the Many* by Michael Eskin (2010 Next Generation Indie Book Award for Social Change)
- *Descartes' Devil: Three Meditations* by Durs Grünbein
- *Fatal Numbers: Why Count on Chance* by Hans Magnus Enzensberger
- *The Vocation of Poetry* by Durs Grünbein (2011 Independent Publisher Book Award)
- *Mortal Diamond: Poems* by Durs Grünbein
- *Yoga for the Mind: A New Ethic for Thinking and Being & Meridians of Thought* by Michael Eskin & Kathrin Stengel (2014 Living Now Book Award)
- *Health Is In Your Hands: Jin Shin Jyutsu — Practicing the Art of Self-Healing (With 51 Flash Cards for the Hands-on Practice of Jin Shin Jyutsu)* by Waltraud Riegger-Krause (2015 Living Now Book Award for Healing Arts)
- *The Wisdom of Parenthood: An Essay* by Michael Eskin
- *A Moment More Sublime: A Novel* by Stephen Grant (2015 Independent Publisher Book Award for Contemporary Fiction)
- *High on Low: Harnessing the Power of Unhappiness* by Wilhelm Schmid (2015 Living Now Book Award for Personal Growth & 2015 Independent Publisher Book Award for Self-Help)
- *Become a Message: Poems* by Lajos Walder (2016 Benjamin Franklin Book Award for Poetry)

- *What We Gain as We Grow Older: On Gelassenheit* by Wilhelm Schmid (2016 Living Now Gold Award)
- *On Dialogic Speech* by L. P. Yakubinsky
- *Passing Time: An Essay on Waiting* by Andrea Köhler
- *In Praise of Weakness* by Alexandre Jollien
- *Vase of Pompeii: A Play* by Lajos Walder
- *Below Zero: A Play* by Lajos Walder
- *Tyrtaeus: A Tragedy* by Lajos Walder
- *The Complete Plays* by Lajos Walder
- *Homo Conscius: A Novel* by Timothy Balding
- *Spanish Light: A Novel* by Stephen Grant
- *On Language & Poetry* by L. P. Yakubinsky
- *Philosophical Truffles* by Michael Eskin
- *The Complete Poems* by Lajos Walder (Bilingual Edition)
- *Összes Versei* by Vándor Lajos
- *The Man Who Couldn't Stop Thinking: A Novel* by Timothy Balding
- *Of Parents and Children: Tools for Nurturing a Lifelong Relationship* by Jorge & Demián Bucay
- *The Impostors: A Novel* by Timothy Balding
- *The Zucchini Conspiracy: A Novel of Alternative Facts* by Timothy Balding
- *Drámái* by Vándor Lajos
- *The Square Light of the Moon: A Journey of Healing with Jin Shin Jyutsu—an Ancestral Japanese Medicine* by Véronique Le Normand
- *On Writing Philosophy: A Manifesto* by Michael Eskin
- *The Spectator: A Novel* by Timothy Balding
- *Gespräch über Deutschland. Mit zwei Essays* by Ulrike Draesner & Michael Eskin
- *Channel Swimmer* by Ulrike Draesner
- *Yoga Town* by Daniel Speck (forthcoming)

Printed in Dunstable, United Kingdom